I0596355

THE CHRISTMAS SLAY

PRAISE FOR WES RAND

"The unconventional collected works of Wes Rand was recommended to me. I can say these are not for the whimsical as you'll wish that only bandits, outlaws, and wildlife, are the only things to fear. Bring a gun as you sit down to read and pray you are not on the wrong side of Major Neville Stryker."

— **DIANE KAWASAKI**, WRITER AND STAR OF TLC'S HIT SHOW MY LITTLE LIFE

"Gritty, dark, and fast-paced—If you love frontier action, Wes Rand's EVIL STRYKER SERIES will knock you out of the saddle."

— *ERIC J. GUIGNARD*, AWARD-WINNING AUTHOR, AND EDITOR, INCLUDING *AFTER DEATH…* AND *BAGGAGE OF ETERNAL NIGHT,* BRAM STOKER AWARD-WINNER

"As a filmmaker, I can see the vibrant images come to life on every page as Evil Stryker crosses every line of decency and yet leaves the women wanting him and the men wanting to be him. Wes has created an anti-hero of devastating impact."

— **VINCENT ROCCA**, WRITER/DIRECTOR OF *KISSES AND CAROMS,* AUTHOR OF *11 SIMPLE STEPS TO TURN A SCREENPLAY INTO A MARKETABLE MOVIE: OR, HOW I GOT A $10K MOVIE TO GROSS $1 MILLION THROUGH WARNER BROS*

"A wild ride through the old west, filled with unforgettable characters and plenty of action. This series hits all the marks! You're going to love Evil Stryker!"

— **JOHN PALISANO,** VICE PRESIDENT OF THE *HORROR WRITERS ASSOCIATION* AND BRAM STOKER AWARD-WINNING AUTHOR OF *NIGHT OF 1,000 BEASTS*

"Payback is Hell operates like a confident, skilled executioner across its violent Western landscape."

— **DALLAS SONNIER**, PRODUCER OF BONE TOMAHAWK

ALSO BY WES RAND

Left to Die

Cross Cut

Payback is Hell

To Die For

THE CHRISTMAS SLAY

WES RAND

THE CHRISTMAS SLAY

Copyright © 2020 by Wes Rand

Cover Copyright © 2020 by Wes Rand

All Rights Reserved.

No part of this book may be used or reproduced in any manner whatsoever without written permission from the author except in the case of brief quotations embodied in critical articles or reviews.

Cover Illustration by Konstantin Yastrebov

Cover Design and Formatting: EditsByStacey.com

Editor: EditsByStacey.com

ISBN: Paperback, 978-1-7362400-0-7

eBook, 978-1-736-2400-14

This is a work of fiction, no resemblance to persons living or dead was intended by the author. Thank you for supporting art.

This is the first printing.

Printed in the United States of America

If you purchase this book without a cover you should be aware that this book may have been stolen property and reported as "unsold and destroyed" to the publisher. In such case neither the author nor the publisher has received any payment for this "stripped book."

❀ Created with Vellum

For my children, Tyler and Anna, and Anna's husband ,Tom,
And especially my wife and partner, Pamela

CHAPTER ONE

All the houses in Pescadero were painted white. It's said they got the paint in from a wrecked clipper ship, the Pigeon Carrier. The little town founded in 1860, lays two or three miles from the Pacific coast, depending on which trail one took to the beach. A peaceful community, surrounded by farms and lumber mills, hardly anything exciting ever happens there.

The man who set out on a brisk morning ride to the beach in December liked it that way. That's why he rested in Pescadero. He kept to himself. Elena, the woman who ran the boarding house, is the only person he talks to. She buys the groceries and supplies, and when asked about her strange boarder, she said she knows nothing about him. He rode to the beach and up or down the coast each morning. When he returned, he had a cup of coffee, read the newspaper, and got a massage from Elena.

It is probably best Elena didn't know who he is or what he is. Her boarder is a killer.

Former Major Neville Stryker spent the last four months in Pescadero. He liked the smell of the sea. Having been born in San Francisco and raised there until age fourteen, the salt air reminded him of home. Only he had no home and no family. At one time he had a wife. Their life together was good. Upon leaving the army, he'd become a successful investment banker with the House of Morgan. Leigh was a beauty from a wealthy family. But it was during an artillery demonstration gone awry when she and her family were killed. Stryker himself was partially to blame for the accident. It happened years ago. The guilt still hung on him like an overcoat he couldn't take off.

Two people have come into his life. One saved it. The other made it worth saving–George Hearst and the Bickford woman.

He had no enemies, none that he knew of. Those he knew occupied graves. They didn't get a second chance.

A tall man, he rose to a full height of six-feet, three-inches. He tipped the scales at a little over two-hundred pounds. His fierce features didn't invite unsolicited introductions. Long black hair, with a few salty speckles having popped up the last year, reached his shoulders. He had a drooping mustache, Mexican style. A week-old beard ran along the jawline. But it is the piercing gray eyes of a predator bird, sunken in above sharp cheekbones, and beneath protruding ledges of heavy brows that ward off strangers. A mix of Asian, Mexican, and European blood, many women found him ugly. Some thought him a curiosity. None said he's handsome.

He wore a .44-40 Colt Peacemaker low on his hip and had a .44-40 Winchester in the saddle boot. The razor in his back pocket was used for shaving, most of the time. However, the weapon he carried behind his back mesmerized dying men, watching their blood drip from its tines. It's called a sai. The three-pronged, handheld weapon is used in up-close fighting. Originally an Asian farming tool, it developed into an effective defense against the sword. Although often fought with two, Stryker carried only one.

The name on his saddle skirt used to read MAJOR NEVILLE STRYKER. Years of weather and use have worn off some lettering. Many say what remained best fit the man–EVIL STRYKER.

He got caught up in the Civil War when he was fourteen. The War, West Point, Indian Wars, Leigh, J.P. Morgan, Leigh's death, all of it seemed lumped together. At the time, each life chapter was isolated. Now, they've aged, and the recollections were all in the same drawer. The bad memories bled on the few good ones, drenching them in blood, and nothing was recalled favorably. Tragedy rode with him since, almost always accompanied by violence. Stryker became like a perpetually wounded animal, snarling and vicious. He lived from one day to the next without purpose or goal. On occasion, he did a job for Hearst. Occasionally, he'd see the woman. Haunted by the past, he survived as if by animal instinct.

Stryker rode the roan-colored gelding up the coast. He followed the trail for five miles overlooking the sand and water twenty-five feet below. The trail wound along the rim through tall grass and bushes. A few trees dotted the landscape far from the beach. Waves rolled in, breaking in regular intervals, sending foamed sea water rushing up the sand. Sandpipers chased the receding waves, hunting insects, sand crabs, or biofilm, a thin nutritious layer left on the sand. In the water beyond the breaking waves, kelp rode in the sea, rising and falling with passing swells. Sea lions popped to the surface, dove, and reappeared several yards away. Seagulls flew low above the water, looking for fish. The fog had not yet burned completely off, and a chill lingered in the salty air. The roan walked at a steady cadence, exhaling frosty puffs of vapor. Stryker took a deep satisfying breath and filled his lungs with the aroma of sea air, wet grass . . . and life.

Up ahead, a stream on its way from the hills to the ocean formed a crease in the land, a crevice that deepened and widened as the creek neared the sea. The trail swung away from the beach and started down a short series of switchbacks. It leveled out along the stream to the beach where the freshwater flows into the ocean. During dry season, the creek lost its strength and died in the sand. The trail disappeared in loose sand and emerged a hundred feet later on the north edge of the little delta. There it started up another set of switchbacks.

It wasn't until Stryker rode down the descending trail and reached the loose sand that he heard the voices. They came from his left, hidden by a rocky bank pushing out toward the sea. The adolescent voices, at least two males, and one female argued. The boys cursed; the female cursed back.

"Hold her arms, dammit!" One of the males yelled.

"Roy! You fucking asshole! Let me go!" The girl cursed.

"Just hold her Eugene til I get her undies off! Shit Reba, stop your fightin'. Ain't nothin you ain't done before."

"Roy! I'm gonna kill you!" Reba glanced right and saw Stryker sitting on the roan fifteen feet away. "Don't just sit there, shoot the fuckers!"

"There's a man over there." Eugene saw him at the same time. He released Reba's arms.

Roy backed off the girl and reached for his trousers lying in the sand. "We just havin' a little fun, mister." He tried to pull on his pants but toppled over.

"They wuz gonna rape me!" Reba, on all fours, ran her hands through the sand searching for her lost underpants. She gave up, got to her feet, and pulled down her skirt. She found her book she'd been reading and cleaned it off with a couple of angry hand swipes. Then Reba stomped through the sand toward Stryker.

Stryker leaned forward, crossing his arms on the saddle horn. Reba looked to be older than the boys, maybe early twenties. Her dirty blonde hair fell down to her shoulders, thin and pretty, she already had a hard look about her. She'd been around.

The boys looked seventeen or eighteen and had a ways to go before manhood. A .22 rifle rested against the bank. "We wuz huntin' ducks an' . . ."

"That's bullshit! You sittin' above me on the bank shootin' sea lions! Fuckin' assholes."

"Where you goin' Reba?" Roy pulled his pants on sitting down.

"Pull me up, mister." Reba reached an up arm to Stryker.

Stryker leaned down for Reba's arm.

A shot rang out. Reba's body jerked, and she corkscrewed to the ground.

Stryker pulled the Peacemaker and fired. Roy took the .44 slug in his chest, blowing him off his feet. He threw the .22 in the air. The rifle landed in the sand beside him.

Eugene looked at the .22 and must have decided it was a bad idea. The man on the horse was fast. Didn't matter, Stryker's second shot killed him.

"Oh . . ." Reba tried to push herself upright. A red blotch on the back of her right shoulder was growing. She finally managed to sit up. "That fucker shot me, didn't he?"

"Reckon so," Stryker agreed. He holstered the Colt.

Reba swiveled her head to see the two bodies on the sand. "Good." She looked up at the mixed-breed. She'd started to raise her right hand but grimaced and lifted the left one instead to shield her eyes from the sun. "My buggy is up on the road."

Stryker dismounted. He helped Reba to her feet and asked, "You ride?" He found a hole in the back of her shirt made by the bullet. With a little more inspection, he saw where the bullet furrowed across her shoulder blade and upper arm. Another bullet hole was an inch off the shoulder seam. "Creased your back. You'll live."

Stryker lifted Reba's left foot to the stirrup and gave her rear a hard push. She almost slipped back, but he shoved her in the saddle. He replaced her foot with his and swung onto the roan behind Reba.

"Roy's daddy owns half of California," Reba said, as they crested the bank. "Go that way." She pointed at a trail running from the beach up to a road on a gradual incline up the hill. Stryker guided the roan onto the trail and Reba added, "He ain't gonna believe a thing neither of us say." She attempted to look back at Stryker. "Ow." She grimaced and faced forward again. "I don't know who you are. Don't care. Grateful for what you did. But I never went down there. I just rode the buggy on that road. Never saw you neither." Reba paused and then continued. "The afternoon tide will come in and sweep 'em out. No tellin' what they'll look like if they ever wash up."

"The wound," Stryker said.

"I fell gettin' out of the buggy."

Stryker helped Reba off the roan and into the buggy. She took off without another word.

Stryker climbed on the roan and started back down the trail to the beach. When he came to the rim trail, he turned south in the opposite the direction he'd ridden up the coast. He thought about why he shot those two boys. The gun was a single shot .22. He wasn't worried about being shot. But they'd fucked up his morning ride.

"Here's your beer and paper, Mister Stryker." Elena held out both, one in each hand. "Be back in hour." She'd come into his room without knocking. Once early in his stay she had waltzed in thinking he was out, and found him completely naked, washing himself. Neither of them acted embarrassed. They just went about their business. Elena never knocked after that. She did suggest he did not need to keep his clothes on for the massage. A towel would do.

Stryker read the *Examiner*, since William R. Hearst now published it. He might have preferred another newspaper, but he made a habit of studying the personal section. It was in that section he'd seen the message from Morgan.

Six months before, she'd put in a notice that George Hearst had a job for him. She'd also written she wanted to see him too. And now he had to admit to himself, he paid particular attention to the personal section because of her. She had everything he desired in a woman, looks, brains, and principles. She made no demands. That would have driven him away. Morgan didn't indicate she wanted a man she could control or tame, and she sure couldn't do that to Stryker. Going to her of his own choosing made it better. Morgan didn't need him either. Her husband was murdered in Bickford two years ago, and she sought no quick replacement. Although she and her husband had drifted apart romantically, they remained close business partners, co-owners of their ranch and mine until he was killed. choosing

The nightmares had come back. Last night, Stryker had another dream where his wife lay bloodied and broken, mortally wounded from an artillery round, one that had landed out of the safety sector during a firing demonstration. Two men were to blame. He was because he hadn't double checked the gun settings, and another man who'd purposely put the wrong settings on the Krupp 75. That man, a business competitor, wanted the demo to fail. Stryker hunted him down and killed him, a murder for which he's still wanted. Leigh remained alive a short time. Stryker found her, and she died with his name on her lips. For years the guilt rode heavy on his shoulders, manifesting itself in nightmares that included the visage of his wife calling his name on bloodied lips. For a while, the dreams had abetted. Now they were back.

And there it was, today in the personal section. He'd had a feeling in his gut it was coming–the reason the nightmares returned? Shit, fucking, God-damn shit. Why? Was Morgan a threat to Leigh's memory? Were the dreams subconscious reminders not to forget her? He had no control over them. They came. They invaded. They haunted. He couldn't stop the damn things.

The notice read, "To NS. GH has another job. Please come ASAP." Strange, Morgan hadn't mentioned herself. Who listed the notice? Didn't really matter. Hearst had saved Stryker's life, and he still owed him. The money the senator paid for the first job eliminated the need for subsequent payments. Hearst paid him $100,000. He would heed the call.

The nightmares though, they put him in a foul mood. And now a mystery with Morgan loomed, a nettlesome annoyance that added to the mixed-breed's foul mood.

The jinx.

Stryker, not one to believe in mysticism, was a pragmatic man with one exception. Throughout his life, anyone one who'd gotten close to him died–often violently. It happened time after time. He'd thought Morgan died too. But she'd survived. Snake bit so often, he figured she wouldn't escape the jinx. It'd eventually get her. He kept Morgan at arm's length.

Stryker packed and rode out of Pescadero that afternoon. It was a two-day ride over the Santa Cruz Mountains to Saratoga and another day's ride to San Jose. He boarded the Southern Pacific in San Jose on the third day, taking him and the roan to San Francisco.

He sat alone on the train. If there was an empty seat other than the one next to him, people took it. Even on a good day Stryker never seemed friendly, and he appeared less so now. His time in Pescadero allowed for needed rest. The coastal rides provided relaxation. But Stryker was not a laggard. He possessed rigid self-discipline, and his stay in the little coastal town had been scheduled with a purpose. His Asian uncle's strict training in the martial arts and years in the Army instilled inflexible habits. He hadn't just grown into it. It was the way he was made. He'd watched his mother and father get slashed to death by union thugs on the Embarcadero when a young boy. Bullies constantly teased and beat young Neville. That is, until his uncle, Sensei Wong taught him how to fight. After Neville killed a boy, it was decided he finish his schooling in the east. The Civil War interrupted that when he was fifteen. However, he completed his education at West Point, and another ten years of the Army followed. Stryker received hard discipline for over twenty-five straight years.

So, Stryker sat alone. He lived alone. He often denied himself things he desired. Morgan was one of those. She asked him to visit the last time he saw her. He never made the trip. Why, he couldn't say. Whether guilt over Leigh, the damn jinx, or some other deep hidden glitch in his mind, he never traveled to San Francisco to see her. He could handle Morgan being upset he hadn't visited. But her death? Shit.

The train rolled into San Francisco's Ferry House station late morning on a warm sunny day, unusual for the city by the bay. Ordinarily, he got to enjoy its cold, miserable, rainy weather. Stryker stabled the roan and climbed aboard the Market Street cable car that carried him to the Palace Hotel. The Palace, constructed in 1875, was the most luxurious hotel in the world. Elevators, in-room baths, multi-story columns, opulent rooms, and the finest restaurants, it was, and still is, a classic landmark, whose guests included presidents, royalty, and the rich and the powerful. San Franciscans boasted half the country's business deals took place within its walls. Simply stepping inside the Palace seemed to make a man feel wealthier. He couldn't be in the hotel unless he had money, and if he's there, well then, he must have money. Stand up straight, push out your chest, and lock your thumbs behind your lapels. You're somebody.

Stryker entered the elegant portal and crossed the paved roundabout adorned with six-foot high potted ferns and four-story white columns. Although he had money, the thrill of wealth, his or that so conspicuous around him, was ignored. He strode through the lavish surroundings, comfortable within himself, a man with authority. He wore it on his hip, strapped low. Money can buy a bullet. It can't stop one. A .44 slug will bore through a fancy suit as easily as a threadbare shirt. And Stryker was fast with the gun.

He stopped at the front desk. The attaché in the green blazer with a gold capital "P" on his pocket expected him. "Sir, the senator will see you in the men's grill room. May I take your bag, sir?"

Stryker swung his carry bag to the attaché's white-gloved hand. *Odd*, Stryker thought, *Hearst always saw him in his room before*. The staff member hadn't called him by name, though. He most likely didn't know it. So, Hearst hadn't divulged that. All fine by Stryker. Secretly meeting another man, even a U.S. Senator, in his hotel room did make him a little uneasy, anyway. The only other men he'd met one on one in their rooms, he'd gone there to kill. But Hearst, a self-made millionaire who'd worked in Virginia City silver mines, was a tough, uneducated man. Rumored to have killed a man in Park City, Utah, he and Stryker held mutual respect for each other. On occasion, the senator had delicate matters which needed handling, situations where discretion had to be exercised, leaving out his name. Resolving those kinds of problems can often be messy—bloody. They require someone with a unique set of skills, skills which Stryker possessed.

The Men's Grill Room was a separate dining area for cigar-smoking men who ate prime beef and drank fine whiskey—no women allowed. On rare occasions a woman might be permitted to dine behind closed curtains at a table booth, especially if the gentleman needed to be discreet. Then, an agreement among the other gentlemen, who at times themselves wished not to be seen by gossipers, would allow a colleague and his paramour a quiet dinner together. And no mention of such rendezvous was ever made, even at the men only tables. Nor outside the hotel, a gentleman's word is his bond. A cavernous dining area with dark mahogany wood, white tablecloths, and velvet green curtains and cushions, the Grill Room exuded formal manliness. Decorum maintained.

"Right this way, sir," the restaurant host motioned with a slight bow. He spun and started smartly down the booths alongside the left wall, coming to the last one, he turned, and extended his arm toward a table covered in white linin inside half-opened forest-green curtains. He saw Hearst seated on a cushioned seat, matching the curtains.

Senator George Hearst sat facing forward. He greeted Stryker with a nascent grin and a curt nod of his head. Craggy face, age showed on a man who'd had a rugged life. With a mop of unruly gray hair and a straggly beard, the sixtyish rail-thin Hearst still commanded respect even though he'd had little formal education. Lively gray eyes clued one he possessed a sharp mind.

Senator George Hearst, father of William Randolph Hearst, had needed Stryker to secure the *San Francisco Examiner* for his son, and Hearst sent soldiers to rescue him from angry loggers in the Big Basin bent on hacking him to death. Stryker got the paper's deed signed over which repaid a poker debt to the senator. The previous deed holder did not survive the transaction.

The host stepped forward and pulled back the curtain.

"Stryker," Morgan greeted him with a smile. She scooted over a few inches, making room for him to sit beside her. Stryker slid in next to her. Morgan Bickford, a good-looking widow, hired Stryker to get her ranch and mine back. He did. He admired the woman as much for her values as he did for her beauty. When the Senator once asked Morgan what she saw in him, she replied simply, "He's killed for me." Stryker couldn't, or wouldn't, call them friends.

"Thanks for coming, Stryker," Hearst said in his usual gruff voice. "Want coffee?" The Senator waved for a waiter.

"Yes." Stryker glanced at Morgan. Their eyes met for a moment. Neither spoke. He turned to Hearst. "What's the job?"

The senator acknowledged the question with a brief smile.

"Trouble up north." A waiter arrived at the table. "Breakfast Stryker? Ours is on the way."

"Coffee'll do." Morgan looked downright fetching, brunette hair parted on the side, white shirt, tan skirt, bronzed arms, strong but delicate hands, and those cheekbones, eyes, and lips–damned tempting.

The waiter upon hearing Stryker's reply bowed again and left.

"Trouble." Stryker said.

"A small mining town in the hills up there–got a letter from the mayor. A girl disappeared. They found her charred body a week later. Now two more girls, one's thirteen, one's fourteen, gone missing. Not sure how to help." Hearst looked at Morgan and then back to Stryker. "I don't think the army is for this right now. Figured maybe you could go find out what's goin' on."

"Name of the town." Stryker said. Morgan edged ever so slightly closer. Her leg brushed against his.

"Johnsville, it's a little gold mining town northwest 'bout forty or so miles from the Truckee area. I've got interest in the Plumas-Eureka mine up there; own twenty per cent of it. The manager, and he's the mayor too, fellow named William Johns, wrote bring heavy clothing; it's roughly a mile high in altitude with snow. Not like Jamison City, a wild mining town half-mile away, Johnsville's very religious. At Christmas time they even change the name of the town to Christmas. I reckon you take the Central Pacific to Reno, then take the rail up to a spur heading west to Mohawk or thereabouts. From there you'd have to travel horseback or sled on up to Johnsville. Consider it a personal favor for me Stryker; I'll still pay you, though."

"Johns got any suspects?"

"No, Bill ain't no lawman, never needed one until now. One thing though, he said there's been some vandalizing of the church and nativity scenes in the yard. Said that was goin' on about a week before the first girl disappeared. Don't know if that has anything to do with it. He just made mention of it."

"There's a Paiute in Carson Territorial Prison, read about him a month ago in the *Examiner*. He killed a white. Name's Tooonug. I want him."

"He kill a friend?"

"No."

"What you want with him?"

"Tracker."

"Tracker." Hearst repeated.

"Yeah."

The Senator's eyes narrowed. "You know this Tooonug?"

"Yes."

Hearst had seen the news article as well but hadn't read it through. The first few lines told of a dispute over horses. He wondered what the real reason was for Stryker wanting Tooonug, but he didn't ask. "I'll see what I can do."

"When will you know?" Morgan had stayed out of the discussion until now.

"I'll telegram Carson City. Say it's important and urgent," Hearst said.

"Your breakfast." Two men wearing short waiter's jackets, and each with a napkin draped over a forearm arrived. One held the tray. The other waiter served from it. He placed steak and eggs in front of Hearst, oatmeal by Morgan, and gave coffee in a cup of fine china to Stryker. It came with a matching saucer, creamer and sugar bowl, all with twenty-four carat gold "P"s on them.

Hearst and Morgan busied themselves eating breakfast. Stryker lifted his cup. Eschewing the tiny handle, he wrapped his hand around the cup and sipped weak, lukewarm coffee. He kept his opinion of the Palace's coffee to himself.

About half-way through his steak and eggs, the Senator said, "Morgan, why don't you show our friend here around the new park, while I place a telegram." He smiled and winked at Morgan. Turning to Stryker, "It'll take a while to get back a reply. Anyway, the next ferry to Alameda leaves in the morning. You take the train to Truckee from there–I guess you already know that, don't-cha. Well, if I don't hear nothing by morning, stop at the telegraph office in Truckee. I'll send word one way or another."

"We have a new park, the Golden Gate Park. It is very pretty and . .

.” Morgan suddenly stopped. “It’s a bit of outdoors in the middle of the city.”

“Take a courtesy buggy from the hotel.” Hearst jammed another bite of steak in his mouth.

Morgan watched the old man cut into his steak. Focused on cutting the meat, Hearst didn’t notice her little grin.

CHAPTER TWO

"Still planting flowers," Morgan said, as the buggy exited under the arched entryway from the Palace roundabout. "Lots of trees, lots of greenery, and they've put in lakes and streams, and buggy roads for viewing. We could've even taken a cable car to it. There are several now that connect with the park. Eventually, there will be other points of interest, a museum or two, and works of art, but for now I think they wanted to make sure the park remained close to nature." Morgan sighted ahead, looking past horse and driver down Market Street. "It'll be a beautiful park, even more so than now. You could've come to see me, asshole. Already people spend a full day just enjoying the natural environment, picnicking, and strolling in it. I like it a lot myself."

Stryker failed to pay attention to anything except Morgan calling him an asshole. He had no excuse really, none she'd understand. Words jumped around in his head and he couldn't get the damn things formed up to march out his mouth.

Stryker sat for several minutes staring at the horse's ass.

"Looking in a mirror?" Morgan quickly went back to the previous subject. "There'll be tall buildings, crowded streets, but I hope the park always survives as a place to escape the city."

"Know anything about Johnsville, Morgan?"

"No, it's a mining town. There'll be miners, probably left over from the gold rush, Europeans; maybe Chinese too, they work the mines. Asians dig the shafts, unlike prospectors who roam the hills searching for gold. Chinese can't stake claims, so they work as laborers, poor devils. They build the railroads and haul ore from the mines. And they run laundries, about all they're allowed to do. George said sixty miles of tunnels surround Johnsville; all dug by hand, most by Chinese." Morgan paused, taking a quick breath. "I think it's a decent size town: churches, saloons, hotels, hardware stores, legal buildings, barber shop, stamp mill–what George told me. Don't know about brothels." She remained looking ahead. "Why you want that Indian?"

"I figure somebody knows who's doing the kidnapping. When I find them–if I find them–Tooonug'll get it out of 'em, before he lets them die."

Stryker would kill too quickly. Indians, especially in the savage tribes, know the art of torture while keeping victims alive. Morgan shuddered, "Perhaps we'll see the new statue being worked on."

The buggy driver turned around. An older man, he was wearing the Palace uniform, forest green coat, black pants, shiny boots, and a top hat, "Ya'll comfortable?"

"Yes, thank you, driver," Morgan raised her voice a little to answer. The horse clopped loudly.

They rode past the last housing structures and over sandy dunes, coming at last to the park's east entrance. The park's rectangle shape, three miles long, east to west, and one-half mile wide north to south, appeared as a geometric forest rising up from the sand dunes. The driver slowed, allowing Morgan and Stryker time to leisurely view the scenery out both sides of the buggy. At particular points of interest, he would halt completely.

"As you can see, Stryker, there's still much work left to do. In fact, I imagine they'll always be planting new trees, flowers, re-routing water features, constantly making changes, improvements, and keeping the park fresh. A little piece of tranquility, right here in the middle of the city. What you think, you like?"

"That statue, there," Stryker pointed with a forefinger. "Driver, take us closer to the statue ahead on the right." The driver swung the horse onto a short path leading to an open turn-a-round in front of a large granite stone holding a bronzed soldier kneeling with a rifle. He pulled up in front of the figure and stopped. Stryker stepped from the buggy. Morgan followed. They stood side by side looking up at the statue. It was a young soldier with a backpack and a bayonet attached to his rifle barrel. Being bronze, one couldn't tell the color of the uniform. The artist had managed to capture the effect of battle on the youth's appearance. The soldier was still in his teens. However, the haggard stare on the boy's face had aged him, aged on the field of battle, not by time.

"What do you suppose he's thinking–war's end, family, home?" Morgan asked.

"Just give me tomorrow." Stryker turned away.

"He'd said that like he knew," Morgan whispered to herself. She remained standing by the statue, studying the soldier after Stryker climbed in the buggy.

"Ma-am, can you spare some money for food?" The scruffy beggar had come around the rear of the coach and approached Morgan from behind.

Morgan jerked upright, startled by the unfamiliar man's voice. She whirled around. The man personified what the end of the line looks like: dirty, red eyed, puffy face, wild hair and beard tangled in knots only scissors could undo. He apparently had no shoes because he was standing on the ends of trousers too long for him. And he reeked of urine, puke, shit, and open sores. If you drenched him in raw sewage, it'd make him smell better.

"No, go away." Morgan backed toward the statue. She scrunched her face. The odor swept over the area in an all-out assault. She briefly gagged.

"What's the matter, lady? Don't like my parfum?" The panhandler lurched forward and grabbed her. He attempted to press his mouth on her lips. She turned away at the last moment and he kissed her cheek. The additional weight caused her to fall. Morgan landed upright on her butt, jammed against the base of the statue. The tramp fell with her, landing astride Morgan's splayed legs. "Ain't you a pretty one." He leaned down for another kiss.

Morgan squeezed her eyes shut and turned her head. "Stryker!"

The man didn't get his kiss. Stryker grabbed a fistful of scraggly hair and yanked backward. He stuck the center tine in the corner of the vagrant's eye and smashed his head against a bent knee. The needle point tine drove through the eye and into the brain. Stryker cleaned the sai on the dying man's clothing and shoved him off Morgan's legs. He stuck the sai in the pouch behind his back.

Morgan opened her eyes. "What a loathsome creature!" She exclaimed, scrunching her face. She scrambled to her feet. "He smells awful! You punched him good and hard. He's bleeding, serves him right. Maybe he'll think twice before he tries that again!"

"Come on, let's go." Stryker threw an arm around Morgan and guided her back to the buggy.

"That man ain't gonna do a lot o' thinking." The elderly driver gave Stryker a quick look, and he let the riders settle in their seats before he slapped the reins.

Morgan had been in the company of powerful men, business leaders, more than one police chief, senators, and several other political leaders, even a vice-president. But she could never feel as safe as she did with the man beside her. At least he had that going for him.

The driver drove on for another half mile before pulling into another turnout by a small lake with a tiny island and a stone building on it.

"Driver, what's over there?" Stryker asked, pointing at the island.

"Not much, I just thought this a pretty view. The city hired them an engineer, a Mista' Hall, and he's in charge of everything in that park."

While Stryker studied the view, he asked Morgan, "Have you been to Johnsville?"

"Jesus Christ, Stryker. Just kiss me."

He removed his Stetson and leaned down to her. Morgan's lips were soft and yielding . . . and inviting. He stayed a while. She circled her arms around his neck. Their lips eventually parted. She kept her arms around his neck, giving him little kisses on the cheek. Finally,

Stryker's arms found their way around Morgan's waist. She felt his strong hands press into the small of her back. They continued holding each other, savoring the intimacy. A feint breeze blew the ends of Morgan's hair off her collar. A soft, tantalizing fragrance wafted up from her neck.

Stryker pressed harder.

Morgan arched back against him. She shifted her lips to his ear.

"Later perhaps?" She whispered.

"Tonight."

"Yes."

They failed to pay much attention to the rest of the park's points of interest.

Only the driver enjoyed the island's view.

Morgan held Stryker's hand in both of hers until they arrived back at the Palace. When the buggy came to a stop in the hotel's interior court-yard, one of the attaché's was waiting for their return, and he marched briskly to the carriage. He stood at attention with his arm extended at a right angle, presenting an envelope in a white-gloved hand.

"The Senator asked me to give this to you as soon as I found you, sir." The attaché waited as Stryker opened the envelope and read its contents. "Shall I carry a reply, sir?"

Stryker put the note back in the envelope. He turned to Morgan. "Shit." Stuffing the message in a shirt pocket, Stryker addressed the courier, "No, I'll see him now."

The attaché dipped his head, spun smartly on his heels, and walked away.

"There's been more trouble in Johnsville," Stryker said to Morgan. "He got the Governor to help get Tooonug. I'm leaving tonight."

Morgan stared at Stryker. Actually, the two of them looked at each other for a few moments without speaking.

"Shall I go with you to see him?" Morgan asked. "And yes, I have been to Johnsville."

They met in the senator's suite on the top floor of the Palace. The two-room suite had thick forest green carpeting, dark mahogany wood paneling, a redwood conference table, and four plush wing-back chairs clustered around a small round table. The second room off to the right housed a bed. Senator Hearst stood smoking his pipe by the window. There was another man with him.

"Sanford, this is Major Neville Stryker, the man I told you about. And also, this here's Morgan Bickford; she's my number one mining engineer." Hearst introduced the two to the second highest office-holder in the state of California, Lieutenant Governor Nicolas. The pudgy politician stood all of five feet. Wearing a gray pin-striped suit, Nicolas had rosy round cheeks which suggested he might be fond of drink. He sported a tidy little paunch which hinted he had trouble pushing back from the table, and a gold watch with a chain on his vest to tell him when to do both. He was one of those men who always seem to wear a smile, a cherubic expression accompanied with a mischievous sparkle in his eyes. The eyes widened when they saw Morgan.

"Please to make your acquaintance, my dear." Nicolas waddled short steps to Morgan, grasped her hand, and bent to kiss it. He didn't bend too much. One, he was short, and two, his belly prevented body bends at the waist. "You'll be coming with us?" He asked.

"No," Morgan replied. She withdrew her hand, wondering whether she should be flattered or amused. She decided on amused.

"Sanford will be going with Stryker to Carson City and then on to Johnsville," Hearst said. "The Indian will be released to them. Nicolas and me, we got his pardon, told 'em in a telegram the Paiute was innocent. He'll go back to Carson if he don't help enough. We'll tell that boy he better do a good job for us." Hearst drew on his pipe.

"Senator Stanford provided his private train, the Governor Stanford, to take us south around the bay, and on up to the line heading over the sierras to Reno," Nicolas volunteered. "It'll haul us down to Carson and back up to the Sierra Valley spur to Mohawk Pass. From there we travel over land to Johnsville, and the senator can have his train back. When we get ready to return, we wire him and he'll send it over to pick us up."

Stryker thought it was good to have friends in high places.

"It's good to have friends in high places," Nicolas said with a wink.

Stryker suddenly looked at the Lieutenant Governor. After studying Nicolas for a bit, he asked, "When we leave?"

"When you're ready, Mister Stryker. There's been another charred body found. That makes two now, and the other teenage girl's still missing."

"Could be sacrificing virgins," Stryker said. The room turned ominously quiet. Senator Hearst nodded grimly.

"My God," Morgan whispered loud enough for the others to hear.

"We'll leave tonight," Nicolas said, his smile gone now.

"My horse too," Stryker growled. He sounded extra gruff, being none too happy about missing out on Morgan's charms.

"We have a horse car, Nicolas replied, whatever you need, sir."

"Let's go." Stryker turned and headed out the door. Nicolas made quick little steps to catch up.

After Nicolas and Stryker left, Morgan turned to Hearst. "Horrifying."

"Bastards!" Hearst growled. "The army would hav'ta abide by a soldier's code of conduct. I'm glad Stryker won't be bound by any such restraints."

"No," Morgan said. "He's not bound by restraints."

Stryker would have closed the door to the rising lift; however, the hotel operator held it open for the little waddling man vigorously rocking his elbows side to side as he *ran* down the hall. "Thanks for waiting, sir," he huffed to the attendant. "Haven't run that fast in forty years!"

His joviality disappeared when he noticed Stryker eying him. The mixed-breed eyes were ice cold. Nicolas shied from the steely slits stabbing him. "Uh, these lifts are something, aren't they?" Nicolas offered nervously.

"Why are you going?" Stryker had no use for a government witness in Johnsville. He intended to find the kidnappers and kill 'em. Tooonug would help, but not this man. And in his mind, killing those in his way didn't matter, even if it meant spilling the blood of a fat politician.

"I go every year about this time. I . . ."

"Lobby, sir," the lift operator announced.

"Sir, if you'll allow me," Nicolas said hurriedly as they exited the lift. "I'll help get the Paiute released." When he received no objection, he almost *ran* to the nearest attaché.

Stryker continued to the front desk to retrieve his bag. An attaché snapped to attention as he approached. "Need my bag. Name's Stryker." The young man whisked about and ran off toward the rising room. *Shit, it's already in the room*, Stryker realized. He shut off the vision of Morgan waiting there and settled against the counter. He watched as the little fat man stabbed his finger in cadence with barked instructions to another attaché.

From the corner of his eye, he saw a young man and woman appear, hurriedly crossing the polished marble floor. They approached from the entrance portal and came directly to the front desk near Stryker.

"Sir," the young man said to the desk clerk, "We need to book passage to Johnsville. It's very important." Some men in their early thirties can pass for twenty. Clean shaven, a slight build, a handsome fresh face, and a buoyant demeanor can make it easy to misjudge the years. Except for the crow's feet by his blue eyes, one couldn't guess the thirty-year-old, blond-haired lad wearing a black shirt and clerical collar, to be much beyond twenty.

The desk clerk, all of five-foot, seven inches of him, stood rigid as if a poker stick was rammed up his implied authority.

Stryker listened as he waited for Nicolas.

"We only make arrangements for hotel guests, sir," the clerk answered icily. Are you staying at the hotel?"

"No, but they told us you made travel arrangements." The girl chimed in, not quite whining, but pleading plaintively.

"Sorry, miss." The clerk defrosted a little. The girl was very pretty. "We have a strict policy against . . ."

"Against what?" Nicolas had finished with the attaché. The cherubic little politician intruded because the girl was very pretty.

"Against booking passage for non-guests, especial-lee," the desk sniped, "on the senator's private train." He obviously enjoyed being snarky.

Nicolas drew himself up to absorb the full measure of the girl's beauty. The blond curly locks swirled about the portrait of a face only Michelangelo could draw. Azure eyes as blue as a Polynesian sea, lips full and rosy pink, teeth white as fresh snow on a brilliant day, a perfect creation on flawless porcelain skin. She wore a blue floral dress matching her eyes. The winsome nineteen-year-old lass flashed a smile that could melt a rattler's heart.

The esteemed lieutenant governor swayed a bit. His knees went wobbly. He clutched at the counter's edge to keep from crumbling to the floor. "Where are you headed, miss?" Nicolas asked, his voice cracking two levels above normal.

"Johnsville, sir," the handsome cleric said. "I've been asked to serve the Lord there."

"I see." Nicolas managed to regain control of his throat. His eyes remained glued on the girl. "You must make travel plans?"

"Yes sir," said the minister. "You see, they are having their annual Christmas pageant next week and the town's other parson—now deceased, he died two days ago—was suddenly called to be with God, heart I hear. I must get there for the candlelight service and all. We just found out the ferry we're supposed to be on tonight has engine trouble, and it won't be ready for another twenty-four hours. The ferry master said the only train he knew leaving tonight was the Governor Stanford."

Stryker remained leaning with an arm propped atop the mahogany counter, passively watching, figuring what was coming next.

"Then you'll join us on the train." Nicolas beamed pompously. "As lieutenant governor of this fine state, it is my duty to care for the needs of my constituents." Turning to the desk clerk, "They'll travel as my guests."

"Who shall I say is accompanying you, sir?" The desk clerk asked. The tinge of sarcasm did not rise to the level of getting him fired, and Nicolas let it pass.

"I believe I've been rude. Would you tell me your names again, please?" Nicolas asked; they hadn't told him before.

"I'm Reverend Venard Dhal, the young pastor replied. Laying a hand at the girl's elbow, he added, "and this is my wife, Luscious." Upon seeing Sanford's eyebrows jump, Reverend Venard explained further with a quick smile. "Her actual name is Lucinda. They started calling her Luscious before I met her."

"Luscious Dhal." Nicolas could barely contain himself. "I'm Sanford Nicolas, Lieutenant Governor." He beamed proudly.

"You bringing the God-damned choir too?" Stryker *politely* asked.

Nicolas and the hotel clerk cleared their throats, and threw embarrassed, apologetic faces at Luscious.

Stryker, still leaning on the counter, gave no hint of humor. The stern look on his face meant he wanted a serious answer.

"No, no one else." Venard seemed to notice the mixed-breed for the first time and stiffened. The pastor gently shoved Luscious toward the counter. He angled his body forward, placing himself between Stryker and his wife. "Sir, are you . . ."

"Mr. Dhal, you are aware of the trouble in Johnsville?" Nicolas asked.

"Trouble?" Venard furrowed his brow. He cast a quick glance at Luscious.

"Don't you know what happened to the other minister?"

"He fell ill? I thought he suddenly took sick and died. No?" Venard replied.

"Not exactly, I'm afraid. He did die suddenly, though. You see, he was attacked two nights ago near his home, and be-headed."

"How awful!" Luscious wailed. Her eyes burst scary wide. She cupped a hand over her mouth.

"Easy, dear," Venard said, wrapping an arm around his wife.

"This man," Nicolas said, hooking a thumb over his shoulder at Stryker, "is going with me to see about that and other disturbances—there's been kidnappings too. His name's Stryker. A military detachment would take several days to organize and get 'em up there. Stryker'll get there quicker and be more effective, I think."

"He looks capable," Luscious dead-panned.

CHAPTER THREE

Stryker failed to make Luscious feel safe. Venard, after much pleading and arguing, persuaded her to climb aboard the train at the Ferry House. Pastor Dhal and his lovely wife sat on a green felt settee at the far end of the governor's plush Pullman coach, away from Nicolas and Stryker. Perhaps his fearsome features reminded her of the savagery in Johnsville. The mixed-breed looked dangerous. Violence hung on him like a dark cloud harboring a bolt of lightning. His ghostly pale eyes glared menacingly, and when he bared his teeth, it was a snarl, not a smile. His whole body appeared ready to explode even when he stretched out his long legs.

Stryker brought the brim of his Stetson over his brow. He straightened his legs, crossed the Hyer boots, and settled in for a long ride. The lieutenant governor took the hint, and he re-located to the settee opposite the Dhals. He brought the *Examiner* stuffed under his arm. Kerosene lanterns on the walls provided flickering light to read. The stove heater centrally located against a wall provided heat, but offered little light. Dark mahogany paneling on the walls looked luxurious with the forest green upholstery and brass fixtures, nevertheless it darkened the coach.

"We're in for a long night," Nicolas said, settling his butt on a cushion beneath a lantern.

"We've not been this way before," Venard said. "Can you tell us how, or what route the train goes?"

"Well, first we swing south to go around the bay to San Jose, and turn north from there. Up through Stockton, and on to Sacramento, then we head east up and over the Sierra's. We get off the train north of Reno and travel by horse or sleigh to Johnsville."

"I haven't seen snow before," Luscious said without enthusiasm. She loosened her two-handed grip on Venard's arm and he swung it around her shoulders.

"You'll see it," Nicolas said, smiling. "Where have you lived where it didn't snow?"

"Los Angeles, we both grew up there," Venard answered. He patted his wife's hand.

"Is he asleep?" Luscious whispered, nodding toward Stryker. She leaned toward Nicolas and used her hand to shield her mouth.

Nicolas shook his head and mouthed "no" at the same time.

"I don't like him. Why did he have to come with us?"

"We might need him."

"He scares me."

"He scares me too," Nicolas whispered, mouthed it actually.

Whatever other questions the girl had would wait. Venard took it upon himself to ask for her. "What do you know about our companion?" He spoke carefully; Stryker could probably hear him above the clacking wheels.

"The Senator, Mister Hearst, has complete confidence in our friend. When he asked the governor if Mister Stryker could ride along with me to Johnsville, he explained the situation had gotten dire up north. Said he needed to get him there as soon as possible. I understand he has unconventional skills, but they're supposed to be effective. I believe we should be happy he's with us." Nicolas glanced at Stryker and breathed a little easier when he saw no reaction from Stryker.

"This trouble, it's been going on for a while?" Venard asked.

"Not too long, I think. Wasn't there last year, and the first I heard of it was from Senator Hearst today."

"It's so dark outside," Luscious said, staring out a window behind Nicolas. She snuggled closer to her husband.

"Yes, it's getting dark early now, isn't it?" Nicolas flashed a smile to the girl. "We'll go even slower at night, checking the rails ahead, you know. When we get to the mountains, there could be snow on 'em, might be delays." Lucious flashed a worried look on her face and the lieutenant governor added, "We've got a good strong engine with a big cow guard on it. Don't worry."

The Governor Stanford was the largest engine in the world at that time, weighing in at 77 tons. Hauling only the horsecar and the tender car–besides their luxury coach–the big engine was plenty strong for the load. Traveling at twenty miles per hour, much of the time the three-cylinder, three-truck engine could normally chug over the narrow-gauge rails with no problem. However, the full strength and wrath of the mighty Sierras in winter lay ahead for the Governor Stanford and its passengers. Winter storms in the Sierras dumped more snow than almost any other place on earth. Twenty to thirty feet on level ground was common, and drifts as high as several hundred feet in others. The deepest recorded drifts in 1890 were reputed to have been an astounding five hundred feet in depth.

"How many men up front?" Stryker let everyone know he hadn't been asleep. A forefinger raised the brim.

"Three," Nicolas replied. "Engineer, fireman, brakeman, snows been light the past few years though."

The Stetson was lowered again.

"Sheds will help too," Nicolas quickly added. "Yes, Luscious." His heart beat faster saying her name. "The railroads have covered much of the higher tracks with wooden sheds, and they help a lot. The men who built the railroad–the big money men, Stanford, Huntington, Hopkins, and Crocker–have more than a thousand men clearing the rails."

Nicolas, satisfied he'd made a good case, picked up the *Examiner* he'd laid beside him. When he opened it in front of him, shielding his face, Luscious canted her head against Venard's shoulder and closed her eyes. The pastor sat rigidly upright, staring ahead.

Eventually, the three of them, including Venard, relaxed, slumped down in the cushions, and drifted into an easy slumber. Stryker maintained an uneasy slumber. A part of his brain remained awake to the outside world, trained by years in the army. He remained vigilant even during sleep. Always a light sleeper anyway, it was one of those traits which kept his mean ass alive.

Clacking train wheels played a monotonous lullaby for the sleeping passengers. When it stopped in Stockton to take on boiler water, they left the train and stretched, and again in Sacramento when they halted for coal and more water. By now they'd been on the train ten hours. Another hour and a half later, they pulled into Auburn as daylight crept in and chased the night sky farther west.

The brakeman's boots thudded on the coach steps, and then onto the platform. He opened the front door and announced, "We'll be at least an hour. If you want a hot breakfast, Frida's, a couple doors down the street on the right, should be open."

"He didn't say it was good," Nicolas said with a yawn. He threw the paper he'd used as a blanket off his body and sat up, swinging his feet to the floor. "Shoulda used real blankets. They got 'em in the cabinet there," he groused and pointed to a built-in cabinet by the front door. "Sorry, kids, fell asleep on you. You'll need them in the mountains."

"It's getting light outside," Venard said, peering out a window. "What town is this?"

"Auburn," Nicolas answered.

"Is it gettin' colder?" Luscious asked.

"A little. We climbed about fourteen-hundred feet. Auburn's a mining town, Placer County, heart of the California gold rush. Most other towns around here died off, this one hangs on. Got lots of miners still working here—rough lot."

Nicolas threw on a hat and coat and waited patiently while Venard helped Luscious with her coat, then he made his way out the rear of the coach. The Dhals followed. Stryker left last. A cluster of buildings grew up by the train depot, a little ways from the main part of Auburn, Frida's café being one of them. The tantalizing aroma of cooked bacon and sausage greeted the four as they approached the café, seemingly making the brisk morning more embracing. A sign was nailed flat on the wall above the door. Stryker guessed everyone knew about the place. Better signage wasn't needed. Nicolas opened the half-lite door and held it for Venard, Luscious, and Stryker. The dining room, about one degree from smothering hot, was already crowded. Stryker estimated around thirty miners, made up most of the diners, Chinese were not allowed in Frida's; they ate in China-Town. The other few customers looked as if they'd stopped in to eat while waiting for another train or stagecoach. A heavy layer of cigarette smoke greased with bacon and sausage wafted about the stuffy room. The rowdy talk stopped when Luscious walked through the door. On the left was a long counter with wooden stools lined up in front. Square wooden tables, with each having four chairs, occupied much of the floor space. Smaller, round, elevated tables without chairs took up some empty spaces. One table against a wall with three chairs was vacant as was one of the elevated tables near it. Nicolas and the Dhals started for the table by the wall; Sex-hungry eyes watched silently as Lucious, with Venard and Nicolas, wove their way to the empty table. After she sat, the banter resumed, but not as loud. Stryker went to the elevated table. He stood next to it, facing the door. Hardly anyone noticed the mixed-breed.

The four of them had finished half their meals when two more men walked in. They could have been miners, except neither of the two had the signs of a miner's hard life. Also, one of them appeared too well fed. He stood five feet, ten inches, and possessed considerable girth. His round face accorded his round belly, a little ball atop a big ball. He sported a short red beard and carried a Navy Colt single-action revolver stuffed in the front of his wide leather belt. He wore black suspenders, apparently in case the belt gave out, and brandished a wide smile. It seemed over-used. The second man was stout but not fat like his friend, and clean-shaven. He had no gun that one could see; however, he carried a large hunting knife in a side pouch. The smaller man trailed his fat friend across the floor. They went to the only available table space–Stryker's table.

"Mind if we join ya?" The big round man asked, showing off crooked teeth in a huge smile. He leaned on the table with weighty forearms, sloshing Stryker's coffee. Some spilled out of the cup and puddled in the saucer. The other fellow was a bit more cautious, standing to the side. No room to lean on the table, anyway.

"I eat alone." Stryker didn't return the smile.

The smile slid from the big man's face. "Here's the only place to put down a plate, mister." He pulled his arms from the table and rose to full height.

Stryker cut into a sausage.

"Come on, Milo. Let's go somewhere else," the second man said. He turned away from Stryker and his table and looked for another table to join.

"All right, Vince. This man don't want our company."

Milo stepped away from the table and looked for another place to eat. He hadn't taken a good look at Luscious, but he did now, and she was staring straight at him. The bull-shitter in him took control. How many men have acted a fool in front of a good-looking woman? He couldn't be cowardly in front of this blue-eyed angel with blond hair watching him. Big Milo was about to add his name to a long list of fools. He allowed himself one last look at Luscious, making heart-stopping eye contact with the heavenly lass, and turned back to Stryker.

Stryker edged right, a slight shift, hardly noticeable. He finished sipping from the cup and sat it on the table.

"We'll take the table. You leave, mister."

Stryker ignored him. He kept his hand around the cup.

Milo's bluster was called. Time to show his gun. He reached for it.

Stryker drew, cocked, and fired the Peacemaker, in what seemed like one single blur of movement. To an untrained ear, the Colt's metallic clicks and roar happened at the same time. So fast, so sudden, so deadly.

The.44 smashed into Milo's chest. He managed to pull the Navy Colt, but the big bullet knocked him backward. Milo and his gun parted company. For a moment it appeared to hang suspended in air. Then gravity prevailed. The Colt fell below the table and clanked on the floor.

Milo staggered onto a table behind him and fell on a stack of flap-jacks. The four miners scraped back their chairs. Two tipped completely over. Too startled to yell or curse as the fat man gasped for air on their breakfast. In fact, after the gunfire no one in the diner said anything at all. Heavy silence pounded the eardrums.

Stryker dug out a silver dollar and flipped it on the table. The vibrating coin made a ringing sound on the wood, breaking the silence. He held the Peacemaker hanging down by his holster and strode between the tables. When he reached the door, he opened it and went outside.

In the cafe, Milo finally stopped gasping.

"Jesus, Milo!" Vince cried, a couple steps away, staring at the dead man on the pancakes.

Those four miners whose breakfast lay under Milo edged closer. The bullet hole in Milo's shirt was neatly centered in a crimson blotch. He rested with eyes squeezed shut, a grimace fixed on his fat face. The wide grin had evidently left to find another bull-shitter.

Nicolas and Venard looked at each other.

"Huh," Nicolas grunted.

"Huh," Venard replied.

Still staring at Milo's body, Luscious didn't hear them. "He's dead, isn't he?"

"Not puttin' up much of an argument," Nicolas said. "Time for us to go."

"Yep." Venard pushed away from the table and got to his feet. "Luscious." He took her elbow and grabbed her coat.

Outside, they spied Stryker getting on the train.

"We don't need delays," Nicolas said. "Let's board."

As the train started its slow roll, Nicolas looked out the window. Two overweight men with badges walked briskly, ran a few steps, and then hustled again toward Frida's. A waiter wearing an apron followed several paces behind them, walking. Another waiter had stepped outside the café, waving his arms. Then the train passed the livery stable, blocking their view.

Luscious stood by Nicolas, looking out the window with him. Venard sat down when he got on. Luscious spun away from the window and saw her husband already seated. He padded the cushion next to him with his hand. But Luscious faced frontward. Biting her lower lip, she took one hesitating step and stopped. Then looking more determined, she marched up to Stryker. She stood facing him; or rather, she stood facing the newspaper. He held it up as he read. The train jerked, and she stomped her foot for balance. She plopped down on the cushion behind her.

"Ah-hem."

Stryker lowered the *Examiner*. He figured the interrupter to be Nicolas. Luscious being there surprised him, but he didn't show it. Figuring she had something on her mind, he folded the paper and laid it across his legs. *Here comes why d'you shoot him?*

"Mister Stryker." The icy stare in the pale eyes caused her to pause.

Nicolas and Venard sat quietly, watching the developing scene at the far end of the coach.

Stryker unfolded the paper, his way of saying get on with it.

"Mister Stryker, I'd like to ask you a few things." She spoke faster now. "Are you going all the way to Johnsville?"

"Yes."

"Will you be staying a while?"

"Most likely."

"I'd like to ask a favor."

Stryker said nothing. He wasn't helping much.

"I want you to protect my husband." She paused again, shorter this time. "I want you to make sure no one hurts him."

"Part of the job."

Satisfied, or at least acting like it, Luscious stood and returned to sit by Venard.

Venard and Nicolas pretended they didn't hear what Luscious had said. They gazed at each other briefly without speaking, and then

Venard asked, "What do you know about the church in Johnsville, Mister Nicolas?"

"Oh, not too much," Nicolas said. "There's maybe fifty or so comes to the Christmas service. Never really spent much time with the pastor there, other than around Christmastime, I mean. The community is more serious about worshipping than most other mining towns. Don't know why. They were pretty regular church goers even before the happenings goin' on there. What I've heard, anyway." He smiled at Luscious.

She returned it as a courtesy. A worried brow kept it less genuine.

"You come up for the Christmas celebrations. They must be something," Venard said.

"Good grief, yes. They even . . . you won't believe this . . . I tell you." Nicolas scooted to the edge of his cushion. "They even change the name of the town to Christmas! Starting on December one, they call it Christmas Town! Decorate the whole town! Candles in the windows, wreaths on doors; they put out a nativity scene with live sheep, sometimes live people too! They march around at night singin' carols, and then on the twenty-fourth, that's when they have the big Christmas pageant in the church. Next day on Christmas they have huge downhill races on snowshoes! Oh yes, you won't have seen anything like it!"

"It sounds wonderful!" said Venard.

Nicolas smiled; satisfied he'd lightened the mood. Even Luscious's face seemed a little brighter. He swung his cheery countenance toward Stryker, reading the paper. That man, he thought, won't join the festivities. *The three of us are going to Johnsville to spread joy, bring happiness. Not him. He'll find the men he wants to find. And when he does, he'll kill 'em—Merry Christmas to you, Stryker!*

Stryker folded the *Examiner* and laid it beside him. He rose and stretched. "Going up front," he said, and he walked out of the coach. Although the train moved at only twenty miles an hour, Stryker took his time stepping over the coupling to the coal tender. The fuel car carried coal instead of wood, a newer fuel source for the locomotive's firebox. A water jacket girdled the slanted coal bin. Steam engines use a lot of water. This tender was enclosed all around with ladders at both ends for the brakeman's convenience, although most brakemen leaped from roof to roof to reach a topside brake wheel in a hurry. Stryker used the ladders. He walked along the roof and climbed down the other side.

"Hey! What you doing, mister?" The "hey" was much louder than the "mister." The brakeman's yell trailed off when he recognized the mixed-breed.

"Snow report." Stryker growled.

"Not bad!" The engineer shouted over his shoulder. Stryker stepped beside him, "Light year, so far," he added. "We'll see how Emigrant Gap is. Gotta a ways to there yet." The engineer leaned out to the side, checking the tracks ahead. "Goin' to Reno up to Mohawk, right?" He asked, slipping back in to watch the gauges. The engineer hadn't once looked at the man he was talking to.

"Carson City." Stryker said.

"Carson City! I weren't told we'd be goin' to no damn Carson City!" The engineer belched in anger, farting at the same time.

"I'm tellin' you now." Stryker said.

"Who the fuck are . . .?" The engineer swiveled around and looked at Stryker. "What are we goin' to Carson City for?"

"Pick up a man from prison. Then you'll take us up to Mohawk."

"Prisoner?" The fireman shouted behind Stryker. "Charlie!" The burly fireman yelled to the engineer. "We're goin' over a hunnert' miles outta our way to pick up a prisoner?" It was really about thirty miles from Reno to Carson City. The fireman exaggerated. Charlie ignored him anyway.

The fireman held the shovel high. He gripped Stryker's shoulder.

Stryker spun and whacked the fireman's grip off with a forearm block. Leaping forward, he circled a fist to the man's temple. At the same time, using his left hand, he grabbed the wrist holding the shovel. Stryker leaped forward and drove his right elbow into the man's chest. Stryker then blasted the heel of his palm up to the fireman's nose. The cartilage scrunched ugly.

Stryker turned the dazed fireman around to face the door. He snatched the shovel and placed a boot on the man's back.

"No!" yelled Charlie, realizing what was about to happen.

Stryker shoved his boot. He turned to the engineer. "Get another fireman."

Stryker handed the shovel to the shocked brakeman and climbed up the tender ladder.

"Any trouble, Stryker?" Nicolas asked when Stryker re-entered the luxury coach.

"No."

"You know, I forgot to tell 'em we're going to Carson City. They don't know we're going there first and then to Mohawk," Nicolas said. "Doggone it."

"I told them."

"Okay, good."

Stryker picked up the *Examiner*.

"Look at those trees. There's snow!" Luscious exclaimed. She sat upright and peered out the window. A light snow dusted the ground. She'd been dozing off and on since breakfast. Venard was reading the bible. Nicolas sat opposite, watching Luscious doze. None of them had seen the fireman in the snow.

The brakeman came through the front door. "We're stopping here in Colfax." He saw Stryker reading the paper but continued to Nicolas and the Dhals. He sat down beside the lieutenant governor .

"Why are we stopping in Colfax?" Nicolas asked. "We don't usually stop there," he said to the Dhals.

"We need a new fireman," the brakeman said. "Sir," he whispered to Nicolas, "are you aware we are headed to Carson City?"

"Yes." Nicolas whispered in return. "Why are we whispering?"

"Do you know why?" The fireman asked, in a normal voice.

Nicolas told him why, gesturing a couple of times at the Dhals as he spoke. The brakeman's eyebrows rose briefly at the mention of an

Indian, however his display of irritation was limited to the brows. Upon learning the full story about Johnsville and the heinous killings, the rail man got to his feet.

"What happened to the fireman?" Nicolas asked.

"Ah, he had a fit when he found out we're goin' to Carson City, and got off the train," he said loudly. "I'll bring on two men. You can get out and stretch your legs, but don't wander off. This ain't gonna take long. The line keeps crews in Colfax." With that, he walked past Stryker reading the paper and out of the coach.

If Nicolas or the Dhals thought it odd, the fireman jumped from a moving train; they kept it to themselves.

The train slowed. The sign on the four-by-four post reading, "Welcome to Colfax, Pop. 657," passed by the window. Years after the California gold rush, Colfax would have died off like other mining towns except for the railroad. Once, an important supply town for miners in Placer County, Colfax was destined to become another ghost town until ten-thousand Chinese laborers laid tracks through it. Now in the 1880s, it prospered as the last hub for men and equipment as the tracks climbed to Donner Pass. A bronze statue of Vice-President Schuyler Colfax stands on Railroad Street in the middle of town. At the time, it was the only known statue of the esteemed politician in North America. Apparently, the VP had visited the town for whom it was named in 1865 (he was Speaker of the House then).

The Governor Stanford rolled to a stop by the statue. Stryker, Nicolas, and the Dhals disembarked and strolled over to read the sign by the bronze Colfax. It read he'd stopped there while inspecting the first transcontinental railroad over the sierras. They'd renamed the town after him, put up the statue, and he'd struck a regal pose for it. The sign also said the elevation was 2,425 feet.

Coming up to Colfax, the hills were blanketed by a heavily wooded forest of pines, fir, and cedar trees, but the town itself had mostly bald hills around it, much of the timber harvested to build the town. The long, wooden depot sat alongside the tracks where the ground flattened between the hills. Main Street ran parallel to the tracks behind the depot on the far side of the tracks. Two hardware stores, six saloons, two hotels, and a bank were cloistered on Main. A barber shop, schoolhouse, courthouse, dental office, church, livery, homes and boarding houses dotted the back streets. The small burg survived the waning mining boom by servicing the trains, providing provisions, tools, and men, especially in winter when the railroads needed ten thousand or more snow shovelers to keep the tracks clear. Workers who kept the rails clear were sheltered in snow shed stations along the tracks, but Colfax served as the primary supplier of tools and equipment on the western approach to the summit. Rails leading up to Colfax lay on a gradual incline. On past the town, the Sierras scaled higher, much higher. Four million years ago, the tectonic forces of subduction caused the oceanic plate to scrunch under the continental plate. The resultant uplifting of the continental plate created a mountain range 400 miles long (north-south) and 70 miles wide (east-west), rising to over 14,000 feet in some parts. The transcontinental tracks crawled over Donner Pass at around 7,200 feet. Lower than the peaks but still high enough to receive almost unimaginable snow.

Venard guided Luscious inside the depot to wait. Nicolas watched them go in. Stryker headed toward a small eatery with a steaming cup of coffee painted on the window. Nicolas peeled off to join the Dhals.

Inside Pritchard's Diner, Stryker took a table in the corner by the window with the coffee cup. Surveying the diner, he saw two more tables; one occupied by an older man with a girl who looked thirteen or fourteen. Another remained empty. A short counter by the back wall extended two-thirds across the floor, leaving a walk-around space between the dining room and behind the counter. The kitchen area was through an open doorway in the back wall. On the countertop were jars of muffins, cookies, and uncut loafs of bread. Stryker saw no restaurant staff. The place was decorated with curtains, flowers on the tables, and landscape paintings on the walls.

Stryker waited patiently for all of thirty seconds before stepping around the counter to find the coffee pot. He found it and poured his own. The man and girl ate their muffins–apparently someone worked in the place–while talking in hushed tones. He was sipping the coffee when Nicolas walked in with a woman. She appeared in her mid-twenties and was easy on the eyes. The man and girl greeted the woman with knowing smiles. They paused briefly by their table and the woman made introductions. He overheard the woman say that they'd be traveling with Nicolas to Reno. Then she turned and came over to Stryker.

Bright smile, white teeth, friendly eyes. She held out her hand. "Mister Stryker, good morning. I'm Jill Sorensen." She pulled it back when Stryker didn't respond. "I'm traveling with the Smith's." She made half a gesture toward the two. "The girl is Lillian Smith. Have you heard of her?"

"No," said Stryker.

"She's the best rifle shot in the country." Nicolas joined Jill at Stryker's table.

"I'll try not to piss her off."

Lillian, over-hearing his retort, put a hand over her mouth to stifle a giggle.

Jill forced another smile. She looked a little nervous. "Mister Nicolas has told me about you. Well, some things anyway. I'd like to hear more."

Stryker gave a steel eyed gaze to Nicolas. The little man fidgeted mightily. He may have been wondering if his relationship with Hearst was enough to keep Stryker from shooting him.

Jill got no reply.

Stryker returned his attention to Miss Sorensen.

Nicolas remained mum.

"He told me you shot a man this morning. Killed him," she said.

Again, nothing.

"I write for the *Wild West Magazine*. I'm doing a story on Lillian Smith, the California girl. I want to write one on you too. I've never met a real gunfighter before." Jill pulled out a chair and sat down. "I understand you may be a wanted man."

"I better go check on the Dhals." Nicolas spun his little round body and fled the shop.

"I understand you killed a man more than ten years ago cause he had something to do with your wife's death. I'd like to hear about it."

His pale eyes narrowed. Anger replaced irritation. The ice under Jill grew dangerously thin.

"You know, one of the things I envy about the young is that they are not burdened by recollections of sorrow," Jill said. "You agree? Say, where d'you get the coffee?"

Stryker rose and returned with a full cup. He placed it on the table, threw down two bits, and walked out of the shop.

"All right then," Jill said to herself, and she drank her coffee at the Smith's table.

Outside, Stryker sought out Nicolas. The little fat politician had probably told the writer everything he knew about him, information surely gotten from Hearst. He couldn't blame the senator for that. Hearst had to. He needed the Governor's train to get Stryker to Johnsville as soon as possible. Still, he and Nicolas would have a talk.

He found him in the depot, more or less hiding with the Dhals. To say that Stryker was pissed would be like terming the Grand Canyon as a small crevice. Stryker figured the sole purpose for Nicolas blabbing to the Sorensen woman was to get the lieutenant governor's name in the magazine. Nicolas probably expounded on his role in the Johnsville mission–print worthy good deeds for sure.

Upon seeing Stryker's anger, Venard and Luscious eased away from Nicolas. Stryker gripped the rotund politician by his meaty throat and dug the razor from his back pocket.

"Stryker!" Jill screamed. She and Lillian with her father came through the depot door. The Smith duo pointed Winchester .44's at Stryker's back.

"Mister Stryker, the train's ready. Name's Levi. Don't wanna pull these triggers, but we will. Me and my girl are pretty good shots."

They filed in the coach car, took up seats with all but Stryker at the rear, and waited for the train to start. When the train began a slow roll, Jill moved up to set across from Stryker. "You weren't really going to kill him."

"Trim his tongue."

"Don't believe that either. Maybe put a good scare in him." Jill smiled.

"Could've gone either way."

"Doubt it, any man who gets his own coffee and still pays for it even if no one's around, has some morals. Not sure where the lines are drawn though," she added.

"Don't write about me."

"Why not?"

"I told you not to."

"Every fool who wants to be in the news will wanna take a shot at him!" Nicolas, overhearing the conversation, shouted from the other end of the coach–possibly trying to get back in Stryker's favor. He also may have realized if his words about Stryker got in print, he might kill him. "Please don't, Miss Sorensen," Nicolas said, shaking his head with pleading eyes.

Jill gazed thoughtfully at Nicolas before returning her attention to Stryker. "All right, I promise."

"We'll be coming to the first tunnel soon," Nicolas shouted, twisting his body and looking out the window. "The tracks are winding up steeper grade. We'll go through two tunnels and then we hit the sheds. We better light the lanterns now."

Stryker got up and struck a match on two of the four wall lanterns. Nicolas lit the other two. Stryker returned to his seat.

"There's trouble where you're going," Jill said. "Johnsville, I mean. That's a mining town in the hills north of Truckee, right?"

Stryker nodded. He was thinking she'd ask about the killings and how he planned to deal with them. Nope.

"Afterwards, assuming you live through everything." Jill flashed a quick smile. "What are your plans?"

"Pescadero. I'll go back there."

"Where's Pescadero?"

Stryker glanced down the coach. The other five, Nicolas, the Dhals, and the Smiths were actively engaged in conversation at that end, talking about Lillian's shooting.

"Southwest San Jose, near the sea."

"What do you do there? What's a typical day for you?"

"Take a beach ride in the morning, come back, have breakfast, read, eat dinner meal, go to bed." He left out Elena's rubdowns.

"You read a lot?"

"Yes."

"Oh, what do you read?" Jill asked, sounding intrigued.

"Newspapers, magazines, some books when I can get them."

"Books?"

"A woman in San Francisco gave me some. She also gave me a few other works to read. Put them in my saddle bag with a note to read 'em."

"A close friend?" Jill veered off topic and followed her curiosity.

"I've killed for her."

Jill tried mightily to hide her reaction. She weltered out a mouthful of words and they piled up on her lap. "You . . . what . . . she . . . who . . . when . . . why . . ." She finally collected herself. "The books, what books?"

"Adam Smith's *Wealth of Nations*, Aristotle's *Treatises on Logic and Reason*, some of his work on the epistemological, Victor Hugo's *Les Miserables*. She gave me a list of other ones. Haven't looked at it yet."

It's difficult to tell what shocked Jill the most, the killing or what he read. "This woman, who is she?"

"Works for Hearst."

"Senator Hearst?" Lillian squealed. "I met him in San Francisco!" She scurried up to sit by Stryker. "He saw me shoot. Said I was the best shot he'd ever seen, man or woman. And I am too!" Lillian boasted. "I can shoot seventy glass balls thrown in the air without missing even one!" She paused, thumped her chest, and added, "Why, Mister Hearst invited me to Washington too!"

Jill smiled politely at the girl.

"You been to Washington, mister?" Lillian asked.

"No."

Jill swung her polite smile to Stryker, and it died.

Stryker's impassive stare at Lillian registered, and it finally dawned on the young shooter. He didn't give a shit. It got awkward.

"Lillian," Levi called out. "Come on back down here, honey. Mister Nicolas wants to hear more about your performances."

"Excuse me." Lillian scooted a few butt widths from Stryker and stood. Turning, she hastened down to the welcome looks of the Dhals, Nicolas, and her father. "He's kinda grumpy," she whispered.

"You performed in Washington?" Nicolas asked. "Tell us about that!"

Lillian perked up. "Yes and . . ." She sat beside her father and recounted in glowing detail the shooting exhibition in the nation's capital.

"What have you learned with your reading?" Jill asked Stryker at the front end of the coach.

"Adam Smith advocated free trade. He said the reasons some nations prosper while others stay poor had to do with free trade. And government interference with high taxes restricts the ability to build capital to buy new equipment and create efficiencies of production." Stryker, not prone to verbosity, felt he had been long-winded here, but he'd recalled and repeated Smith's research accurately.

"This is in *The Wealth of Nations*?"

"Read it." Stryker said.

"I'm not sure if I agree with him. I think it's our responsibility to help our fellow man, especially those less gifted, less fortunate."

"Take from those with ability and give to those with need." Stryker said.

"Exactly!" Jill's excitement suggested she'd made Stryker see a new compassionate social model.

"That's horseshit. Saw a town destroyed with it."

"The people were too selfish?"

"They acted with reason. You should read Aristotle too. When men are gifted money for no work, they don't work. When those who worked, keep little or no money, they stop work–logical."

"There should be laws . . .!" Jill protested.

"Laws don't legitimize theft. A turd with lipstick is still shit."

"I can see you don't care about . . ."

"Actually, I do more than you. You think just because you take a man's money and spread it around, you've done good. You haven't. All you done is make yourself feel good. Nothing more. You haven't helped the man gifted the money, and you sure as hell haven't helped the man you robbed."

"How hasn't it helped?"

"Morgan told a story. A woman in a kitchen . . ."

"Morgan?"

"Mining engineer works for Hearst–a woman in the kitchen saw a cocoon spinning outside her window. Feeling sorry for the struggling butterfly took a razor and slit the cocoon. When it got out, it couldn't fly. It never did fly. The effort of beating its wings against the cocoon builds up the strength it needs for flight. Now go back and sit with the others, and leave me alone. If you write about me, I'll kill Nicolas . . . and you." Stryker rose, left the Stetson on the cushion, and marched to the rear of the coach. Nicolas and Levi, who'd been leaning forward talking with each other, had to suddenly sit back to keep Stryker from hitting them. He slung the door open and walked out.

"Where's he going? Is he leaving?" Jill asked, returning to the group.

Nicolas, watching Stryker through the door's glass, watched him hop to the horsecar and climb the ladder. "He's checking his horse."

"On the roof?" Luscious looked at him too.

"The horse car has a clerestory roof. He can see inside from the top." Nicolas settled back in the cushion seat.

"How did your talk with him go, Miss Sorensen? Nicolas asked.

"Not well. It ended badly," Jill huffed, crossing her arms, and sinking into the cushioned backrest. "Other men just leave a girl crying."

"How's that?" Nicolas asked.

"He said if I wrote about him, he'd kill me."

"You believe him?" Luscious sounded incredulous.

"I'm not writing about him."

Stryker hung on the ladder and stretched high enough to look for the tunnel. The wind was biting cold, and he squinted to see up the curved tracks. Not in sight yet, but he had to hurry. He climbed on top and crawled to the middle. He lay flat and peered through the glass. He saw the roan and scanned the other stalls as well. Directly beneath him, the stall was empty except for a large sack stowed in one corner. He hadn't noticed it before. It had a rope tied at the top and it looked full, oats or grains he guessed for the horses. Stryker then satisfied the roan was okay, rose to all-fours, and crawled back to the ladder.

"Horses all right, Stryker?" Nicolas asked, as Stryker came through the door.

Stryker ignored the question and walked past them. He sat, swept the Stetson off the cushion, threw it on his head, and canted it over his brow.

A little while later they came to the first tunnel. The coach went suddenly dark, dimly lit by the four lanterns. Loss of daylight was replaced by an assault on the ears. The roar of the engine reverberated against the tunnel's granite walls. The hammering pistons and steam bellows no longer dissipated in the open space. The Governor Stanford, seemingly angry at be confined in the tunnel, took out its wrath on the walls. Then a few minutes later, the roar lessened, and it got light again.

"It was a short tunnel, but it took a long time to drill it," Nicolas said. "The Chinese were only able to chisel through thirteen inches a day, even using dynamite. Nitro-glycerin increased it to seventeen inches, but they kept blowing themselves up with it and had to go back to dynamite. We'll be hitting the sheds soon. There's a few short ones at first, 'fore we get to the big one 'cross the summit."

The engine slowed even more than its pedestrian speed of twenty miles an hour winding up steepening grade. Then came a series of wooden snow sheds, built on the tracks where avalanches had occurred or were likely to occur. Apparently, the Stanford wasn't as annoyed being in the sheds; the wood absorbed engine noise better than granite, and although still loud, the roar wasn't as deafening. Not quite as dark either. Where there was no snow piled up outside the shed, cracks between the wooden planks and constructed view windows allowed in some daylight. Nevertheless, whether in the tunnels or sheds, conversation in the coach waned because talk was too difficult to hear. Eventually, they entered a shed that seemed to go on forever.

"This is the long one over the summit," Nicolas yelled. "When we come out of this one, we'll have gone through all the tunnels too. About twenty more miles to Truckee."

"How long is the tunnel?" Venard yelled back.

Before Nicolas could answer, the brakeman appeared at the front door. "We'll be stopping at the summit for a bit until they clear tracks ahead. There's a hotel you can wait in." He turned and slipped out the door before he got any questions.

"James Cardwell built a fine hotel on top, the Cardwell Hotel," Nicolas shouted. "Tell you more later." Shouting was too much of an effort. It could wait.

The engine began decelerating, hardly noticeable at first due to the lack of outside landscape to reference their speed. That meant they'd reached the summit. They'd also gone through five tunnels. The Stanford came to rest a few hundred yards west of tunnel six, huffing huge billows of steam as though out of breath from the climb. Stryker was the last to step from the train and, with one of the firemen, walked back to the stock car to inspect the horses. The other passengers hurriedly shuffled the few feet of covered boardwalk from the tunnel to the hotel. Inside, they were met by a staff member who led them to the cavernous two-hundred-person dining room for snacks and drinks while they waited.

Stryker brought the roan out onto the station platform and down the ramp. Snow had been shoveled out from the hotel, giving the big horse room to walk. As he led the roan back into the car, the train engineer approached to inspect the horses as well.

"How long's the wait?" Stryker asked. He tied the rope from the roan's headstall to the ring on the wall.

"Could be awhile, maybe be rolling by tomorrow," Charlie answered, sounding somewhat guarded.

"Why the hold up? Stryker growled. The fireman, who had been standing next to Charlie, eased back a few steps.

"Earl, he's in bed sick. He drives the bucker."

"Bucker," Stryker said.

"Bucker engine, it's got the plow on it." The engineer noticed Stryker's scowl. "To clear the tracks, we use a bucker plow on front of the engine. Big curved plow used to lift and move snow from the rails. We hook as many as fourteen engines together behind the bucker, get up speed, and ram the snow." Charlie talked with more confidence now. "Sometimes they'll hit the snow goin' fifty miles an hour."

"Uh, and if it's excitement you want, take a ride in the front engine with the plow," The fireman wryly added. "We've lost a few."

"A few," Stryker repeated.

"A few men," Charlie said.

"Earl is the only man to do it." Stryker growled.

"Ain't too many volunteers lately," the engineer said. Sometimes there's more than just snow in the snow, boulders, trees, a frozen body—came right through the window. Fact is Earl's the best. He can read the snow like nobody else, and he gets the speed right. He'll study an avalanche, judge what might be in it by where it came from, and how packed the snow is—how frozen an' such and decide the number of engines and what speed to use."

"Where's Earl?" Stryker asked.

"In there in bed." Charlie nodded toward the Cardwell, looking relieved.

Stryker brushed Charlie aside and stepped across the platform. He burst through the doors to the hotel. Inside, he marched through the dining room to the desk clerk. "Earl's room!"

The clerk must have figured whatever Stryker wanted with Earl was between them. "Ground floor, hall behind you, room 126."

Stryker headed down the corridor, counting room numbers until he came to 126. He entered without knocking. Actually, his size-twelve boot smashed the door open. Earl sure enough lay curled up in bed. He snorted once and resumed snoring. A sparse room even for railroad workers, it had a single bed that jutted out from the back wall. A small nightstand with a lamp was by the bed. An undersized desk with chair was to Stryker's left. An empty bottle of Yellowstone Bourbon sat on the desk. The straight-back chair by the desk held soiled clothing. A half empty glass of the bourbon sat on the nightstand. Stryker moved alongside the bed. Crouching, he gripped the bed rail and flipped it. It was heavier than Stryker expected, and it required a strong leg push. Not all that tall, but Earl carried an extra forty pounds in his gut. He poured onto the floor, yelping like a kicked dog.

Fat Earl landed on his back and laid on the floor, apparently trying to decide which way was up. After figuring it out, he blurted, "What the hell? And who the fuck are . . ."

Stryker stepped across the overturned bed, drawing the Colt. He kneeled and jammed the barrel in Earl's mouth, the front sight chipping a tooth on its way to his throat.

"Clear the tracks." Stryker cocked the gun.

Earl wisely nodded yes.

Stryker took out the Colt and pressed the barrel-end against Earl's forehead—right between the eyebrows. "Talk."

"Ain't no trains coming through til tomorrow afternoon." Earl thought about shoving himself up to a sitting position. He reconsidered.

Stryker stood. He kept the Colt trained on Earl. "Got a train out there. You're gonna clear tracks for it."

Earl sat up now. He gingerly poked a finger where a good tooth used to be. Blood dripped from his chin and pooled in a red flannel undershirt. Luckily for him, the color was a close match. "You could've asked."

"Could've."

"Where's the blockage?" The "b" rode out in a bloody bubble. "Jesus, mister."

"Find it."

"If 'tween stations Stanford and Champion, it's passed the sheds. Let me up."

Stryker holstered the Peacemaker. "Throw on your clothes and let's go." He swept the shirt, coat, and trousers from the chair and tossed them to Earl.

Earl, still woozy from the booze and the rude awakening, sat on the chair to get dressed. "I've had better mornings," He groused.

"It's late afternoon. Hurry up."

"Can I get some coffee?"

Earl finally wrestled his boots on. Then Stryker grabbed his collar and wrenched upward. The front collar tightened on his throat, and he struggled to his feet.

Stryker dragged Earl down the hall. When they came to the dining room, he pulled him over by Nicolas and the others seated around a dining table. Some were eating soup, some were eating sandwiches. All were drinking hot drinks, coffee–or chocolate, as in the case for Lillian.

"Hello, Stryker. Won't you join us?" Nicolas asked cheerfully. Then he saw Earl behind Stryker with a bloody mouth. "Is he all right?"

"Earl's offered to clear the tracks."

Stryker grabbed the cup with the most coffee–which happened to be in front of Levi–and handed it to Earl. Levi didn't object. "Here's your coffee."

Earl took it in two hands and brought it to his mouth. He then spilled half of it when Stryker yanked him forward. Earl managed to take two sloshing sips by the time they got outside. "I hope the drift's on straight track," he muttered when they came out of the hotel.

Stryker looked at him.

"Rammin' a curve ain't no good. T'ween the shed and Stanford station's a curve. Straight t'ween Stanford and Champion. Let's hope that's where it is." He stared back at Stryker. "Either way, I need more engines."

"Where are they?"

"In the engine house." Earl pointed to a row of large wooden buildings on the far side of a larger circular domed building. It stood next to the track where the Governor Stanford rested. "We'll pull 'em out, turn 'em, and line 'em up behind the bucker. I figure six, which means I need six more engineers. I'll go get 'em. If any are sleepin' you can wake 'em." Earl paused. "You ridin' with me?"

"Yes."

"Tell your man to back up. We'll need a quarter-mile track," Earl said. "Can I go get the other drivers now?"

"I'll go with you."

They found the other drivers playing cards in room 130. Stryker, satisfied Earl was committed to the track clearing, joined Nicolas and the rest in the dining hall. Levi had gotten more coffee.

"I was just telling our friends about the hotel," Nicolas told Stryker as he pulled out a chair. "Ole Cardwell built this place in 1870. They say this dining room is the largest from San Francisco to Ogden." Nicolas raised his arm in a wide sweep. Actually, not all that wide. The little fat man had short arms. "He used to have magnificent summer and winter balls in here. Had a bear to entertain the guests for a while," Nicolas chuckled. "Anyway, he sold in '87, or '88. It went bankrupt and I think a couple of brothers bought it. Used mostly for railroad workers and their families now, I hear. Want something to eat?" A waiter came up behind Stryker.

"Coffee and a ham sandwich," Stryker ordered. The waiter spun smartly and left with the order. "Clearing the rails, board soon," Stryker said, loud enough for all to hear. The remaining conversation drifted from one topic to another. Stryker stayed out of it. When his sandwich and coffee arrived, he ate in silence. Jill and Lillian limited their talk to between themselves, while Nicolas chatted with Venard and Luscious. Levi watched the irascible Stryker eat his sandwich and said nothing. The dining room began to shake. In fact, the whole place shook, as the first of the locomotives was brought out from the turntable shed onto the tracks by the hotel. Inside the dining hall, conversation ratcheted higher above the outside rumbling. It was convenient having the trains right outside the hotel, but they sure rattled the plates.

Stryker finished off the sandwich and drained his cup. "Nicolas, come with me." Stryker got to his feet and headed outside.

Nicolas glanced hesitantly around the table with a sheepish grin. He rose and followed Stryker.

"Ain't he the lieutenant governor?" Levi asked, watching Nicolas go down the exit hall. No one answered.

The bucker engine came out first. Earl eased it to a stop in front of tunnel six, a hundred yards from Stryker and Nicolas on the hotel stoop. They stepped off the stoop and watched for another engine to back out of the turntable. Their own engineer had been told to move his train. The Governor Stanford was backed a few hundred yards down the tracks.

"I'll ride the bucker engine," Stryker shouted to Nicolas. "Tell Charlie, to follow with the Stanford. Get everyone on board when they get the sixth engine out. "

"You sure you can clear the rails?" Nicolas yelled back.

"No!"

"I'll ride with you."

"No!"

"I really want to!" Nicolas shouted.

Stryker pushed Nicolas around and toward the hotel. "Ride your train. I'm in the bucker. Don't need you."

An hour and a half later, Earl, Burl, the fireman, and Stryker stood in the cab of the bucker engine. The steel plow blade attached to the front was enormous. Slanted rearward, it had a horizontal wedge to lift snow from the tracks. Above it was a vertical wedge for pushing snow aside. It was like riding behind a building. Five more engines, each with an engineer and a fireman, lined up behind them. No need for brakemen on this job. The six engines sat rumbling by the hotel, rattling its windows. One might have thought the hotel would crumble to the ground before the six iron monsters started toward the tunnel. Earl used hands signals to sign the engineer behind him. That man signaled in turn after him, and so on down the tracks. The engines slowly pulled away, and the Cardwell stopped shaking.

"We'll go slow until we get to the avalanche," Earl yelled. "It's just past the Stanford station on straight track. He's Burl," Earl added, evidently meant the fireman.

Stryker stood behind the engineer and out of the fireman's way, shoveling coal. The bucker engine crept into tunnel six. Except for the firelight coming from the firebox, everything turned black. The noise was deafening. Three of the engines had entered the tunnel. Earl watched gauges and worked the gears. The fireman shoveled coal. They acted as though they didn't hear the furor. To Stryker, everything in the cab shook, the floor, the walls–his head. Hell, even his balls shook. *Shit*, he half expected the tunnel to collapse. Stryker wondered if the two were deaf, but then remembered he'd already talked with Earl. *Damn, a man could shout as loud as he could and wouldn't hear himself!* He began to think he'd made a mistake coming along. Another engine got hooked up behind them and they inched forward. *Couldn't they've hooked up outside? How long is this fucking tunnel?*

Tunnel six was the largest of its kind in the United States, 1,659 feet long. Boring through solid granite was no big deal. It only took working six days a week, twenty-four hours a day, advancing fourteen inches a day–two years to build. The Chinese did it, working in groups of forty. One held the bit and two pounded on it with eight-pound sledgehammers. The bit holder turned it one-quarter turn after each strike so that the hole was bored round. A stick of dynamite was placed in the hole when deep enough. And all done by candlelight. No big deal. One had to wonder how the bit holder was chosen.

Stryker suspected they normally loaded the engines outside the tunnel. Maybe he'd shoot Earl later.

Eventually, they got all six engines on the tracks and hooked together. Then Earl started them off at ten miles an hour and they finally emerged from the east end of tunnel six. Stryker noticed no hand signals were used in the tunnel. That meant this tunnel hook-up was pre-planned, or Earl could tell they had the six coupled by the number of times he felt the locomotives bumping together. They weren't in daylight long before entering another snow shed. The snow sheds went for miles. Earl held them at ten miles an hour. Six engines don't stop on a dime, Stryker figured. Finally, a small light appeared ahead and grew into an arched opening of daylight. Then they came out of the sheds. Where the mountain fell off to the north, the view was stunning. In areas where snow couldn't find purchase on the steeps, huge granite boulders punched through the white blanket. The sierras are strong mountains, granite, hard granite, the source of its strength.

Beyond the mountains, stretching out to the east, Donner Lake lay shimmered blue against surrounding snow.

They rounded a long curve and saw the avalanche four hundred yards ahead.

"There it is." Earl said. There was no whooping. He flag-signaled out the window and slowed the engine. He brought it to a complete halt fifty hundred yards from the slide. "Grab a shovel, mister," Earl said to Stryker. He pointed to a short rack of shovels. We've got a little digging to do." Earl must have felt the train was his province. "I'll survey what it's gonna take to clear. Burl here will show where to dig."

Earl walked briskly ahead of Burl and Stryker. The engineers and firemen from the other five engines joined with their shovels. Ahead of them, Earl climbed up the wall of snow twelve feet high, and disappeared from sight.

"Tell me about the digging." Stryker rapped Burl, a head shorter than Stryker, on his arm.

"We dig out the bottom so the plow don't ride up. Hollow out a ledge. The blade slides under. Dumps snow on top. Weighs the plow down. If'n the plow rides up; the wheels come off the rails."

When Stryker and the shovelers reached the avalanche, Stryker drove the shovel blade in the snow, using it as a pickax and climbed on top. He slipped several times, cursing his slick boots. Hyer boots are good for horse stirrups, or killing cockroaches in corners, but not so good in snow. Stryker made a mental note to get new boots with rough soles. He scrambled to the top of the avalanche and found Earl standing on the far edge. He stepped in Earl's tracks to reach him.

"Be dark soon. I'd rather go back and tackle this in the morning," Earl said when Stryker reached him. "It's two, maybe two-hundred and fifty yards across. Right now, it's still soft. Be frozen hard in the morning though."

"That slope," Stryker said, eying the area above the avalanche. "Trees on it?"

"Not too many as I recall." Earl replied.

"I'm in a hurry."

"Figured as much." Earl ran a finger over his gums. They'd stopped bleeding.

They high stepped back in their boot marks. The holes were deeper now. Coming to the twelve-foot drop, Earl sat and pushed off. Half sliding, half falling; he landed hard on the rail ties and plunged face down in the snow. Another engineer helped him to his feet. Stryker dropped the shovel below and shoved off. The sun had been down for over a half hour now and the snow had firmed. He hit hard but kept his feet.

"Okay, boys, let's bust it open," Earl announced, after inspecting the ledge. "We'll back 'em up past the curve and hit the straight with all we got." Turning to Stryker, he added, "We probably should come back when the light's better and bring the Chinamen. Sure you can't wait?" When he got no answer, Earl took off walking toward the engine . . . with a slight limp.

It'd become fully dark when the men climbed back on the trains. A fireman from the third engine leaped on the ground with a lantern. He scrambled onto a wagon-sized boulder and flashed the light in a circle; did it twice to make sure the signal to back up the trains was seen. He hopped off the boulder and got aboard. When they'd backed up past the long curve, the fireman jumped off again, struggled up a snowbank and waved the lantern back and forth to stop the trains. He waited to make sure all was ready. The six engineers leaned out of their cabs for the next signal.

The lantern flashed again. The signalman yanked the lantern up and down. He quickly slid off the snow and clambered aboard. All six locomotives started forward, gaining momentum as they came around the curve.

In the lead engine, Earl shouted to Stryker, "You better grab on to something." The huge plow in front of the locomotive prevented Earl from seeing when they'd hit.

Five . . . ten . . . fifteen . . . twenty . . . thirty . . . forty miles an hour, they reached top speed. The six engines strained to maintain full power. The fireman slammed the firebox shut, dove to the floor, and braced his feet against the bottom. Earl remained standing, gripping the handles. He braced one foot in front of the other. Stryker hooked an arm around a window strut and braced his feet like Earl.

The explosion of snow was enormous. It blasted through both windows. Massive icy waves swept him off his feet and buried him.

Stryker struggled upright about the same time as Earl. The snow came up to his chest.

"God-damn! That was a good one!" Earl whooped. "Is Burl still in here?" He looked around the cab for his fireman.

A mound of snow in the corner began to wiggle. Finally, two hands broke through, then two arms and a head. "We get through?" Burl asked, blowing snow out of his nose.

Stryker had a new respect for snow buckers.

"Stay inside. I'll see where we are." Earl crawled out of the cab and up on the white blanket covering the engine.

"You boys all right up there?" A man shouted from the second locomotive, also buried in snow.

"Yeah!" Earl yelled back. "Hold tight. I'll have a look see." He trudged ahead in the snow. Stryker lost sight of him as he disappeared into the night and decided to wait. A few minutes later, Earl returned. "We busted through about two-thirds," Earl shouted. "Let's back 'em up and hit it again!" Then he more or less fell into the cab. "We gotta shovel some of this snow outta here." Stryker helped with the shoveling.

"You ready to back up, Earl?" The lantern man called a few minutes later from a snowbank.

"Yeah, go ahead with the signal," Earl yelled, short of breath and leaning on his shovel.

They backed up to where they'd started the first run. Now Stryker knew what to expect. It made it worse. Same explosive impact and the snow knocked the shit out of them again. And although it flooded the cab as before, Stryker saw a dark void outside the window and few stars in the distant sky. This time, they'd punched through.

"Tell your friends to follow us when we start down again," Earl said to Stryker. "We'll back up to the top and you can get off. We'll wait til you're ready."

Stryker helped clean snow out of the engine cab. When they'd finished, Earl's man signaled with the lantern. Earl had done his part, Stryker thought, he'd cleared the tracks. He'd done so even after being thrown out of bed and having his teeth re-arranged. There were times when he could have disappeared and left Stryker, but he didn't. As he studied Earl now, working the gears, watching the gauges as captain of the train, Stryker realized this man was doing his job. His work, it was more important than anything else, more important than Stryker and whatever Earl felt about him. Resentment, revenge, hate, all pushed aside to run his train, clear the tracks.

Stryker thought of his own life, and the jobs he'd taken for Hearst. He did them with no pay. Sure, he'd been paid for the *Examiner*, got paid enough to live on for the rest of his life. So why did he keep working for Hearst? A good question, but when focused on a job, the task at hand, it took his mind off Leigh. Nightmares he couldn't control. When he was awake and idle, her memories—especially the bad ones, came back. They invaded his mind and brought him down, way down. He immersed himself in work, driving himself furiously, angrily, at times. Anger, he held deep-seated anger, anger at himself for letting Leigh down. It was his failure to re-check the gun coordinates which partially caused Leigh's death—*my mother-fucking, God-damned, failure*. His fault.

The signalman jumped from the train and waved the lantern to stop the engines. A rising moon threw off enough light for Stryker to see the hulking shape of the Governor Stanford two-hundred yards up the tracks. Stryker dug a twenty-dollar gold piece from his pocket and handed it to Earl. "Get your teeth fixed."

Stryker hopped off the bucker, walked back to the Stanford, and climbed in the cab.

Nicolas, who'd stayed in the cab, greeted him. He moved away from the doorway, giving Stryker room to step in. "They got it cleared?" Charlie turned to Stryker as well, eager to hear good news.

"Yes."

"Wonderful!" Cried Nicolas.

"Follow 'em. Not too close," Stryker told Charlie. "Avalanche is 'bout two-hundred yards wide. Punched through twice but snow might be falling in."

"Saw you hit it a couple times," Charlie said. "Wondered if you made it through," He shouted to his fireman, "Fire it up, Amos."

"That Earl's a good man. He'll get us through." Charlie turned his attention to the gauges. He leaned out the cab window and let the huge locomotive creep forward. The third pass of the bucker engine went considerably slower and without any snow explosions. The six engines rolled through the cleared passage in the avalanche without a problem.

CHAPTER FOUR

Senator Hearst sat behind his broad mahogany desk. It was in his office at Sacramento, the state capitol. He hated being there. The state provided the office for him—a small one. His abhorrence of the place was well known, and state officials spared expenses. Hell, he could barely squeeze around his desk. The senator liked big stuff. Big and bold, that's how he lived his life. He took big, bold risks in the mining industry and got rich doing it. He'd bought the desk before he saw the space, had it delivered, and the facility's manager held it in the warehouse until his office became available. "The bastard, he knew the desk wouldn't fit in here." Leland's office was three times the size of his. Senator Leland Stanford provided train service to state officials and got special treatment in return. Regardless, two days and he'd be back at the Palace in San Francisco. The office did have a window, and Hearst was looking out at the expansive lawn when he heard a knock on the door.

Governor Waterman opened the door and came in without waiting for the senator to answer. "George, how the hell are you?"

"Bob, I'm old. That's how I'm doing." Hearst knew the governor and liked him, even though he was a Republican. Hearst himself was a Democrat, but their political positions were not that far apart. Like

Hearst, the governor had a history in mining. Waterman had prospected for gold on the Feather River not far from Johnsville and mined silver near Barstow. He made over a million dollars in the mines. "Let's sit." Hearst scooted out his chair and sat with a groan.

"Have you heard anything from your man up in Johnsville?" Waterman asked straight away.

"No, don't expect to for a while." Hearst chose not to tell about the last two missions Stryker performed for him. He'd heard nothing until the jobs were finished. Even afterwards, he didn't learn much. He found it best not to ask too many questions of the man given to solving problems with guns and blades.

"Nicolas telegraphed me from Donner Pass last night." Waterman pulled a cigar from his coat pocket and slowly ran his fingers over it, feeling for lumps. "Said there was snow on the tracks. Thought maybe you heard if they got through."

"Ain't heard a thing." Hearst opened his desk and pulled out his own smoke. He bit off the end and spit it on the floor. After sticking it in his mouth, he lit the end with a match, rotating the cigar over the flame for an even burn. He took three good puffs. "What's on your mind, Bob?"

Waterman lit the cigar. He took his time and got a proper burn before asking, "What you know about this fellow, George?"

"Not a whole lot." Actually, Hearst knew a considerable amount about Stryker. He'd used his official resources and learned Stryker was a former artillery officer, an investment banker for The House of Morgan, and that he was wanted for murder after he killed the man primarily responsible for his wife's death.

"Heard he shot a man in Auburn," Waterman said. The Governor stopped with that and waited to see if Senator Hearst would have anything to add.

"Well, if he did, he must have had a good reason." Hearst drew on the cigar.

"Somewhat self-defense, Nicolas said. Over breakfast, in a café, a man threatened him with a pistol."

"He's good with a gun, I hear."

"You heard right. Very fast, and he doesn't take a lot of time making up his mind on when to use it. George, I've got fourteen militia, armed soldiers, boardin' the train this morning for Johnsville. Thought you might want to know."

"You tell Nicolas?"

"Sent him a telegram. Don't know if he got it."

"Beholden, Bob. Reckon I'll be headin' back to San Francisco tomorrow. Be at the Palace. You let me know there if any news comes your way. I'll do the same."

"Uh, George," Waterman said, rising to his feet. "I appreciate you sendin' that man up there for me. Maybe this'll get straightened out before long, one way or another."

"Hope so, Bob." Hearst rose with a groan and squeezed by his desk to see the Governor to the door. He slung an arm around the Waterman's shoulder and said, "Give Jane my best, will you?"

"And you to Phoebe." Waterman turned to his friend. "We're getting pretty damn old, George."

"Yeah."

Neither man smiled.

On the train to San Francisco the next day, Hearst sat alone in the Pullman ruminating on Stryker's dark side. He pondered on it for several minutes and then shifted his thinking to reflect on Stryker's lighter side for comparison. A sudden epiphany struck the senator. *There is no lighter side.* He remembered he'd never seen the man smile. Both sides were dark. No, only one side and it was pitch black— with occasional streaks of red. *What the hell does Morgan see in that man?* He's killed for her, she said one night. *Surely there is more to it than that for her.* Hearst himself was a callous man, worked hard all his life. Cheerfulness wrung out of him by the harsh years. Ruthless? Yes, he could be ruthless in business. Stryker, on the other hand, could be fair in business, more than fair, and yet ruthless when killing. *There's the difference*, he thought.

Well, anyway, he remembered. Phoebe's in Europe with William. *Why not ask Morgan to dinner?* The senator's mood brightened.

On the downhill run in the Sierras, Earl drove the bucker engine with the heavy plow. The linked locomotives followed as they passed through the last of the sheds and past Donner Station. Truckee now lay ahead with clear tracks the rest of the way.

Behind the plow engines, Stryker in the Governor Stanford was growing more impatient. "They'll pull off to a siding track in Truckee. Pass 'em and go on to Carson City," Stryker yelled at Charlie. "Stop in Reno. Throw the shooter girl and the other two off the train."

Charlie chanced a peek at Nicolas, who nodded yes.

The railroad tracks curving down from the Sierras brought Truckee sputtering to life in the 1860s, known then as Coburn's Station. In 1868 Coburn was discarded and Truckee became the official name after a friendly Paiute Indian guide. Population had grown to about two thousand. The Chinese, which at one time had the second largest Chinatown in the west, had been run out of town. These days in the 1880s, Truckee was a logging town. Not quite as raucous as Bodie, but Truckee did its best. It had all you'd want in a wild west town, plentiful saloons, a red-light district on the infamous Jibboom Street, and nightly gun fights.

Stryker would have liked to spend a few days in Truckee, enjoying himself, but a sense of urgency prevailed. Punching through the snow delayed them several hours and a gray dawn had melted the night away. The Stanford rolled to a stop in Truckee. They took on water, dropped Lillian, Levi, and Jill on the side of the tracks, and then chugged out of town, heading for Carson City. They left the foothills of the Sierras, traveling northeast to Reno, some thirty miles away, and then due south to Carson City, another thirty miles. By the time they reached Carson City, the day had aged to mid-afternoon.

The Nevada Territorial Prison lay isolated, about a mile from the center of town. Nicolas sent a porter hustling for a buggy while he and Stryker waited inside the station with Venard and Luscious. The Carson City Train Station was moved comfortably away from the new Virginia–Truckee roundhouse. Upgraded to accommodate pin-striped politicians, it had comfortable chairs instead of benches. A coffee urn warming over a lit candle rested on a linen-covered table. Overturned coffee mugs sat in neat rows on a tray beside the urn. Beside it, another tray held a teapot and cups for the female passengers.

"This shouldn't take long, dear," Nicolas said to Mrs. Dhal.

A two-story building, rebuilt with stone from a nearby quarry after the original prison, first used as a hotel, burned down. The gray rectangular stone blocks in the interior as well as the exterior made the prison cold and foreboding. Not many prisoners escaped, Stryker figured. He and Nicolas were met at the front door by a short, stout guard who snapped his movements with close-order-drill precision.

"I'll need your gun, sir," He said to Stryker, holding out his hand, palm up. When Stryker handed it to him, he led the two men down a dimly lit hall where he ushered them into the warden's office. Pressly C. Hyman's name with "Warden" printed underneath it was on the door. The warden stood behind a very plain and old, desk with nothing on it, facing a large glass window that looked out into the prisoner's exercise yard.

"The Lieutenant Governor of California, sir," the guard announced, and he closed the door behind Nicolas and Stryker.

Hyman, a bearded stern-looking man, did not greet them with a smile. He eyed Stryker for a long fifteen seconds, before asking, "What can I do for you, gentlemen?" He sat in a swiveled chair behind the desk. His arms were folded across his chest. He made no offer for his two visitors to be seated in the straight-back chairs across from him.

"We're here to pick up a prisoner by the name of Tooonug," Nicolas said flatly. "Sit down, Stryker." He scraped up a chair behind him and plopped down.

Stryker also scraped a chair, lifted it and jammed it on the wooden floor with a resounding thud. Then he sat as well. His pale eyes returned an icy stare to Hyman.

"Lieutenant Governor, sir, why is it that I release this man?" Hyman shifted his attention to Nicolas. He unfolded his arms and placed both palms on the desk.

"Governor Waterman, our governor in California, sent your

governor here in Nevada, Charles Stevenson, I believe, the telegram request for a pardon." Nicolas reached inside his coat pocket and withdrew an envelope. "This is a handwritten copy of it. Underneath it is Governor Stevenson's telegrammed reply." He leaned forward and laid the envelope between Hyman's hands. "Governor Stevenson agreed. In Governor Waterman's telegram it told how the Paiute did not steal the horses. In fact, the men he killed were attempting to steal the horses from him."

"I see," grumbled Hyman. "I wonder now." Hyman re-folded his arms and leaned back in the chair. "Where'd the Injun get three saddled and branded horses? Don't seem right he'd come to own them legal like. You know what I mean."

"Afraid I don't know that, Mister Hyman," Nicolas said, sounding exasperated.

Stryker pushed up from his chair and strolled around the desk. He stood by the window, gazing out.

"My guess is he stole 'em. So, the Injun stays where he is." The warden glanced at Stryker, then turned back to Nicolas. "I'll talk to Governor Stevenson. I'm sure he'll agree with my assessment on the matter," Hyman smirked.

"I gave him the horses," Stryker said, turning toward Hyman.

"You?" Hyman asked with eyebrows arched.

"You did? Yes, that's right, you did," Nicolas said. He didn't sound convincing.

"Three men ambushed us in Utah. I kept the horses." Stryker drawled.

"And they just let you do that?" Hyman asked sarcastically.

"They were dead." Stryker's eyes tightened to slits. He sidled away from the window and leaned on the warden's desk, close to Hyman now, facing him. "Get him."

"Ahem." Nicolas cleared his throat, trying to get Stryker's attention.

"Get off . . . ." Hyman hesitated. Fear pushed authority aside. He picked up the envelope, opened it, and read the letter inside. He recognized the California Governor's official stamp, "The Great Seal of the

State of Nevada," at the bottom of the letter. It was genuine. Nicolas was most assuredly who he claimed to be. And the man next to him made him nervous. He'd admitted killing three men. "John!"

The guard outside the door opened it and stepped inside.

"John, go bring prisoner Tooonug to me. The Injun in cell 14."

Stryker pushed up from the desk, turned and faced the door. Hyman remained seated.

Ten full minutes passed. The warden's door swung open. In walked Tooonug, his wrists handcuffed. The Paiute stood a tall and proud five-feet-four. A wiry man, he had long straight black hair, a grim straight line for a mouth, and eyes as black as obsidian. A tan, weathered face meant he'd spent most of his years outdoors.

"Come closer, Tooonug," Hyman ordered.

Tooonug stepped forward, giving no sign he recognized Stryker.

"I heard a man gave you the horses you stole." Hyman's words dripped with sarcasm. "Who now, gave them to you?"

Tooonug remained silent for a few moments. Then he raised his cuffed hands and pointed at Stryker. "That man."

"We'll be going now, Warden Hyman." Nicolas pushed himself to his feet. "I'll be sure to have Governor Waterman express his appreciation to Governor Stevenson. I'll tell my governor how helpful you've been."

"Take off his cuffs, John," Hyman said, sounding none too happy.

Stryker retrieved his gun from the gate guard. Nicolas and Stryker shared the buggy's driver seat, and Tooonug sat behind them as they rode back to town.

"You had me worried there for a minute." Nicolas snapped the reins. "Git up!" He looked over his shoulder at the Paiute. "Friendly fellow," he said to Stryker. It was getting colder and Nicolas eyed gathering clouds coming in from the west. "We should find a store here in Carson; buy heavier clothing and some provisions–use the state's money," He said, grinning.

"What sizes does he . . . uh . . .?"

Stryker pulled the Peacemaker. Squinting one eye, he clicked the cylinder, checking rounds.

"I guess I can get close enough." Nicolas let it go at that.

They rode the rest of the way to the center of town in silence. At the far end of Main Street, between Calvert's Livery and Ruby's Restaurant, they found Cina's Emporium. Stryker silently mused, how many stores does this Cina man have? He'd seen another Cina store in Bishop, California, a few months earlier. Nicolas hopped from the buggy and stepped on the single plank to the boardwalk entrance. The emporium was a two-story wooden building, freshly painted white with green trim. Stryker climbed off the buggy. He leaned against the seat and crooked an arm over the backrest. He stared at the stoic Paiute for a moment.

"Need your help" Stryker said.

Tooonug gave an almost imperceptible dip of his head.

"Tracking, and might need information from a man who doesn't want to give it,"

A second head dip. Here was a man who was almost verbose as Stryker.

With that, Stryker pushed off the buggy and went into Cina's. Wooden bins stuffed with of all kinds of clothing, hardware, cookware, gadgets, and just about anything a man could want or need to ranch, farm, or prospect—except maybe women—filled the heavily-oiled wooden floor. No women were in the bins, perhaps they were in the back room. Finer household items could be found on the second floor. Upstairs showcased toiletries, women's clothing, sewing materials, enough particulars to make women giddy. A sign over the back door read "Heavy Equipment Outside." The store was crowded and noisy. Cina knew his business. Stryker found Nicolas in the rear of the store's first floor, going over a list of items with a salesclerk.

"We should've brought a wagon," Nicolas told Stryker when he walked up.

"Have it delivered," Stryker said, surveying the surroundings.

"Figure the bill," Nicolas said, returning his attention to the clerk. "Charge it all to the governor's office, State of California. I'll sign it. I'm Lieutenant Governor Sanford Nicolas and deliver everything to the train depot. Hurry now and be quick about it." Nicolas issued the order in his most official authoritative voice.

"I'll have to get approval, sir," the young clerk, a lad of about twenty-five, replied. He looked a bit nervous.

"Add a Winchester .44, two boxes of cartridges, and a sharp knife," Stryker added.

"Go ahead," Nicolas agreed, nodding to the young man. The clerk scurried off to find someone to approve his big sale.

"For Tooonug, I guess?"

"Yeah."

"We get everything within the hour; I think we can be in Mohawk by late afternoon. We'll have to hurry. I saw clouds coming in from the west." Nicolas took off, working his way between the bins to the checkout counter in front. Stryker followed. Aisles ran front to back and side to side, like a checkerboard. Side aisles were narrower. Customers shopping in ones, twos, or threes, sometimes more lingered in the open floor space, causing Nicolas to have to work through clumps of people crowding the aisles. Store staff, all four of them, remained stationed near the front, presumably to make sales, help customers carry out purchases, and to ensure items were paid for.

Christmas shoppers jostled each other in their efforts to find bargains. As Stryker worked his way through shoppers carrying items for purchase, his height allowed him to see over shorter customers. Ahead, by a flat table displaying carpenter tools, two boys in their late teens were horsing around as they picked up work implements–hammers, screwdrivers, chisels, wrenches–and with them pretended to joust . They were having great fun. The boys wore long, heavy wool coats over sweaters and denims. Stryker shifted around a woman with three children as he watched the jousting. A quick sleight-of-hand movement caught his eye. It seemed out of place, like a fart at the dinner table–not part of the fun. A few seconds later, it happened again. One boy facing the front of the store and the clerks, with his back to Stryker, jousted with two chisels, one in each hand. He lunged in jest at the other boy. He extended the chisel in his left hand as in a sword thrust. The chisel in his other hand went around his body, inside the coat. His hand came back out empty.

Stryker, now standing by the fake combatants, saw the one closest to him reach for a hammer. Stryker gripped the boy's wrist and jammed it against the table, flattening the hand. Snatching a needle-point awl from the table, Stryker drove it through the kid's hand.

The boy shrieked in pain. He stared horrified at the awl impaling his hand. Then he screamed again, louder in a higher pitch, like a girl.

Stryker grabbed a short-handled sledgehammer off the table and struck the awl. The blow seated the handle against the young thief's hand. It all happened in less than two-and-a-half seconds. The other kid ran. He passed two male clerks fighting through the crowd toward his injured buddy. They ignored him. The screaming lay ahead.

"What happened?" The first of the two clerks asked Stryker, who was now heading to the front. Other shoppers stopped to stare, craning their necks, searching for the source of screams. Those closest to the impaled boy watched him shriek and tried to figure out how the kid had stabbed himself.

"Check his pants and pockets," Stryker said to the second clerk.

Nicolas saw Stryker and raised his arm.

"What's going on back there?" Nicolas asked when he walked up.

"Some kid was stealing and got nailed."

"Let's pay for this stuff and go." Nicolas waved for the clerk, weaving his way toward them, arms loaded with coats. "You have the voucher for me to sign?"

"Yes, sir." The young man dumped clothing, boots, rifle and shells on the counter and fished the paperwork from a smock pocket. "I had a wagon brought around from delivery. They'll haul this and the rest to the station."

"Good, thank you, young man." Nicolas snatched the voucher and read it. "Need a pen, son."

The clerk threw his hand behind his ear and pulled a pencil. "Here's a pencil, sir."

"Good for you, good for me." Nicolas signed the voucher with the pencil.

Buggy and wagon waited outside, the wagon parked behind the buggy along the boardwalk. Tooonug hadn't moved. The Paiute personified stoicism. Stryker made eye contact with him and then scanned the sky. Streaks of sunlight shone through scattered gray clouds overhead. Angry black ones were gathering over the Sierras to the west. A gathering wind blew from the same direction and he canted his Stetson into it.

"Meet you at the train station," Nicolas shouted to the wagon driver as he stepped from the boardwalk and into the buggy. It had no footstep, and the boardwalk made getting into the buggy much easier for the pudgy yet cherubic politician. Stryker climbed in from the other side.

"Hold on, mister!" A stout man, maybe five-foot, nine-inches tall, hatless with hair simply cut to three-quarters height that never saw a comb, ran out the door. He had a hard look about him, with the kind of face that would break off if a smile ever appeared uninvited–and one never got invited. He wore a brown suit. He was a businessman.

He shuffled across the boardwalk to the buggy. There he stopped, feet splayed, hands on hips. He snorted and spit. "You stabbed one of my customers," he said, directing his attention at the mixed-breed.

"No, he didn't. He was . . ." Nicolas sputtered to a stop. He turned to Stryker. "Did you?"

Stryker nodded.

"That boy had two hammers, four screwdrivers, a pair o' pliers, a chisel, a belt, and a bow tie stuffed under his coat. Name's Cina, an' I wanna offer you a job. Need a good security man."

"Got a job," Stryker said.

"Well, all right, I guess," Cina grunted. "The big thieving is done by them damn politicians. 'Mister Cina, we need a new jail. Mister Cina, we need a new schoolroom. Mister Cina, we need this. We need that.' And if I don't give 'em money, the bastards raise my taxes to get it." His jaw muscles twitched. His face grew puffed and red. He looked ready to explode.

"We'll make sure you get paid promptly, sir." Nicolas snapped the reins.

CHAPTER FIVE

In an abandoned mine shaft, a few miles south of Johnsville, and up on a hill, a group of eight people, five males and three females, squatted around a cooking fire. Outside, a makeshift barricade of pine tree branches and holly bushes guarded the entrance. It also had the effect of diffusing smoke from the fire so that a person passing by wouldn't notice the smoke. He might smell it if he came within a hundred yards or so, but he wouldn't see it.

There were nine people in the mine. The ninth was standing, bound and gagged to a support beam farther back in the shaft. He would not share in the food.

The eight eating by the fire were all young, in their late teenage years. One of the boys called himself Mesiah, or the annointed one. He's the group's spiritual leader. The man tied to the beam was his father.

They didn't live in the mine. There was a shack down the hill, near a stream which served as home. That is where they slept, anyway. They did most of their eating there as well. But today they cooked soup in the mineshaft, a special kind of soup—opium boiled in alcohol, or laudanum. They were about to become *enlightened*. Blankets lay spread on straw matting around the cooking fire, and two lanterns hanging on support beams provided flickering light.

Mesiah provided the ingredients for enlightenment from Chinese dealers in Truckee. Enlightenment meant enhanced euphoria and sexual pleasure, and a psychological-spiritual state of mind. It also caused sexual dysfunction and constipation. That was okay because in a little while they wouldn't give a shit.

"What are we gonna do with *him*?" One of the girls asked, staring at the boiling pot on the fire.

"It will be revealed in time, Willow. God will send a message. Then we must do as he commands," Mesiah said. Willow wasn't the girl's real name. Mesiah gave her the name when she joined as a disciple. He gave all of them new names, names rooted in nature, names to signify them as children of the earth, pure and enlightened. The girls, Willow, Fawn and Dawn, were sisters. The boys were called Leaf and Dale, names of the forest. Wallace and Phil had yet to be given names by the Mesiah. The girls joined Mesiah because they were stupid. The boys joined to fuck the girls. Another two new members remained at the shack near Mohawk. They stayed behind to guard the shack and horses. They'd also run afoul of the annointed one. The boys wanted to fuck the girls. That was against Mesiah's rules. The new kids must prove themselves first.

Mesiah fucked the girls in two's or three's, or whenever he chose. The boys were allowed one girl at a time, and only once a week. Mesiah wouldn't have the boys at all, but he needed the muscle. He rewarded their cooperation with drugs and sex.

Before Mesiah became the annointed one, he was Jack Butcher, Carl Butcher's only child. Jack's mother died at childbirth, and Carl never forgave his son. The whippings, beatings actually, were administered with rage. Jack received the full wrath of his father for being the cause of his mother's suffering and subsequent death eight days after childbirth. For years, young Jack never knew the real reason for the brutal beatings. Then when he was ten, he found out. It was during one of those whippings that Carl yelled at Jack, accusing him of killing his good wife, Martha. Carl would never admit he beat the good wife too.

Martha, a dutiful woman, withstood the beatings. "She deserved them." That's what Carl told her. She was a shamed woman. For what, she never knew, except that she displeased Carl.

Carl had a small, crooked penis. Martha was the only woman who would marry the man, a first-class asshole. She'd never been with another, and she knew no better. Carl took out his frustrations on his wife, and when she died on him, he turned to beating the shit out of Jack. That quite possibly had something to do with Carl being tied to a mineshaft beam with a rag stuffed in his mouth.

Back in the Methodist Church, Carl was a God-fearing man, a regular in the front pew, and a deacon. He worked as a butcher during the week and said amen's on Sunday. Jack, who also learned the butcher trade growing up, sat in the back row at church. That is where he met Fawn and Dawn, whose real names were Sally and Allie, sisters two years apart. Away from his father, Jack was a different boy. He craved acceptance. He craved affection which he'd never had. Never knew he missed it, but when a girl on the back row held his hand at fifteen, he wanted more of that. Shy at first, he soon learned how to impress. As Jack neared eighteen, he'd become a damn good-looking young man with flashing blue eyes, slicked-back blond hair, and at a trim six feet. It didn't take much coaxing to get a girl in his arms. He'd also learned the best places to tickle.

And one other rite of passage swung home to life in his favor. A well-executed right punch sent Carl over the couch. Every father who's had a son knows there comes a time when his boy can whip his ass. He either accepts it or he gets his ass kicked. Carl figured one punch was enough. Jack took a giant leap forward in self-assurance. It showed. Other kids started looking up to him, and Jack was on his way to becoming Mesiah.

Adulation, the final element. Adoration from the fairer sex instilled confidence as well, and that led to sex. Adulation provided power and control. It was intoxicating. Jack began to teach, quote from the bible, and train. Years of forced bible study demanded by Carl began to pay off. Jack took biblical passages and twisted them to suit his purpose. At first, it was to impress. And he did impress. So much so that girls, and boys too, listened to his lectures, believing Jack knew a better way to salvation, one which allowed for a more natural, more enjoyable life here on earth. Of course, he used that spiritual superiority to persuade girls to believe they could live a more purposeful, and at the same time a more natural life as God intended by sucking him off.

Jack's head (and penis) swelled. He felt masterful. And to bring his small group of devotees closer to God and nature, he gave each of them new names, names which emanated from the forest, or nature. At first, Jack was hesitant to bring boys into the fold, but he had a gut feeling he might need their help, especially after his mind began swirling with new ideas, grand ideas. Why not a new church? One where he was its spiritual leader? He asked the group to come up with a name for himself. He rejected ones suggesting the forest, or meadow, or water, or any name for that matter, without exaltation connected to it. Finally, one of the girls came up with Mesiah. Jack beamed. He'd been crowned.

Last night, in the small hours after midnight, Mesiah led five cult members to his father's house in Johnsville, dragged him out of bed, and brought him to the mine shaft. Although Mesiah hated his father, he still had a lingering respect and reverence for the man. He represented teachings of the church, its strict discipline and morality. Those principles and morals nagged Mesiah. They hindered him, caused him to stumble at times, and prevented greater achievement. He had to cut himself off from the church and any connection to it. That connection was Deacon Carl Butcher, his father. How to do that, he hadn't yet figured out. Mesiah was being truthful when he said he'd be given a message. He hoped for one anyway. Maybe the soup in the pot would help.

The laudanum was nearly ready. The opium powder had soaked in water for three days and macerated with alcohol for three days more. Mesiah now percolated the mixture with more alcohol. He took the mixture from heat and let it cool. He knew the others were growing restless, and he blew in the pot as he stirred. After fifteen long minutes, Mesiah poured very small equal portions into nine cups and passed eight to the waiting hands of Willow, Fawn, Dawn, and the boys. He thought for a split second to pour a ninth for his father, chuckled to himself, and decided not to. His production process was crude, even dangerous, as three girls who'd recently died from it could testify. That was if they still lived. Mesiah burned their bodies. He did it as ritual and to hide the bruises and bloody faces. The three girls had fought hard against their first ingestion of laudanum. On occasion, Mesiah, with help from Leaf and Dale, had to force a new member to take it. But after the second, or third time, or sometimes even the first time, force wasn't all that necessary. Laudanum is highly addictive.

"Just sip it!" Mesiah warned when he spied Dale starting to drink instead of sip. "Careful, take your time and enjoy."

Minutes passed. Each person re-situated himself, leaning back and settling into a more comfortable, relaxed, position. Dale and Leaf stretched out, resting on one elbow with Dawn and Fawn snuggled in. Wallace and Phil were only allowed to sit back against support beams and watch. The girls leaned against the reclining boys. Mesiah and Willow cuddled together as well. Now, they all could take delight in the elixir, and each other.

Sex came easy, leisurely, in the drug induced stupors. Frequently, partners were exchanged by simply crawling from one to the other. There was no talking; only silent, slow-moving swaps. Mesiah would often stop and vicariously enjoy the permissive sex. An orgy, it was driven only by pleasure. Homosexual sex blended seamlessly with heterosexual coupling as the twin stimulants of drug and desire smudged constraint. Laudanum, and the sex with it, gave him power over the group. Sometimes Mesiah would take deep breaths, long, deep ones, as though he inhaled power itself. Better than sex. Power even gave Mesiah hard-ons.

When spent, an *orgyant* simply rolled over, offering a rectum if someone else wasn't quite satisfied. But eventually, satisfaction or exhaustion settled on them, and they ceased moving, fully unwound, their bodies resting blissfully against, or on each other.

Four to six hours later, sobriety crept in as laudanum drained out. Limp and aching penis's and sore vaginas–and rectums became more noticeable as the partyers drifted back into reality.

"My ass hurts," Dawn grumbled. She received no consoling words, though, as she watched the group untangle. Each had his own discomfort to content with. Besides, they were bone tired. Let it be known, however, as with many recreational stimulants, after continual use of laudanum, penises don't inflate, and clitorises don't engorge–so much for great sex with drugs.

"What about him?" Dale asked, meaning the man standing bound and gagged twenty feet away, and who had watched it all. "Why'd we bring him here?"

"Can't let him go, Mesiah," Leaf added.

"I know that," Mesiah answered in a low voice. He couldn't sound weak. A decision must be made.

"Maybe we give him the preacher treatment," Dale offered. He said it as a joke. But by the time the words traveled the short distance from lips to ears, they arrived as no joke.

The preacher had been a mistake. But his kidnapping was intentional. His killing was intentional too. His beheading wasn't. It started with a drug-infused ceremonial stabbing of the minister. It took place in the same mine shaft. Each of the cult members were to pass by the bound minister and stab once until he died. However, somehow the preacher freed himself and fought for his life. A powerfully built man, he fought hard but had only his fists as weapons. Someone, one of the boys, grabbed an ax and swung it. The blow nearly decapitated the man. They wrapped the body in a tarp, dragged it from the mine and brought it to a hill overlooking Jamison Creek, on the far side of the stream from Johnsville. That's where the body was found the next day.

Although the preacher's near decapitation was by accident, the deacon's, if it happened, would not be. Mesiah knew what Dale insinuated. "Treatment," that meant cut off Carl's head. Message? Maybe he *should* send a message. Not only to the devout citizens in Johnstown, but to his followers as well. Mesiah glanced at his father. His hatred of him stemmed not only from the brutal beatings. It also emanated from the church and its religion that got rammed down his throat. Years of sitting in the pew, having the preacher condemn, shame, and denigrate him year after year after year, every Sunday, every revival, and every other gathering, gnawed on him for his entire life. At first, he accepted he was a sinner, a despicable sinner who must constantly ask God for forgiveness. The merciful God who would redeem him and allow entry into paradise, whatever, wherever that was. He was supposed to grovel and shake with fear, seeking repentance in front of that damn preacher who seemed to always direct his sermons at him. It started out as a small seed, a question, deep inside. *Why? Why was his mother taken at birth? Why did he not have the gentle hand of a mother all the past years instead of the angry fist of his father? How could a good and merciful God do that to him? What had he done to deserve it?* The preacher's sermons, seemingly aimed his way, taught it were his sins causing the misery dumped on him. It laid on him, heavy around his shoulders, smothering and oppressive. The seed of doubt grew over the years. Then resentment was born. It, too, was tiny at first. But it grew. It grew into anger. It grew into hatred. Hate—he hated the preacher. He hated the church and its teachings. The preacher used to beat him too. But the preacher didn't use fists or belts. He used words, words that cut, and words can cut deeper than a belt. *And that preacher won't be spouting no more of his shit. He won't because his fucking head's cut off. And now it's time to put an end to the God-damned shit coming from that bastard tied to the beam.*

CHAPTER SIX

The three of them, Stryker, Nicolas, and Tooonug, rode the buggy with the wagon of purchased goods following along later. Nicolas drove the buggy to Carson City proper and up Carson Street toward the depot. A few snowflakes sprinkled from a darkening sky, hardly noticeable to the three men in the buggy.

Venard and Luscious waited patiently in the coach of the Stanford. It had been over two hours and the young couple probably worried that they'd been abandoned. Luscious saw the wagon coming first. Venard, sitting with his back to the window, studied his Bible.

"I see them!" Luscious jumped to her feet. She practically leaped across the aisle to kneel beside Venard and look out the window. She waved at the approaching wagon with what she could now see held three people, but she dropped her arm. "I don't think that's them," her voice trailing off near the end.

Venard sat the Bible on the cushion next to him and twisted around to watch the wagon too. "I don't recognize 'em. I'll go out. Stay on the train. Keep out of sight." Venard stood up and took a couple of steps toward the door before stopping to come back for the bible. He stepped off the train with it held noticeably against his chest.

"Good day, sirs." Venard greeted.

"G'day," The man in the middle, holding the reins, returned the greeting with little enthusiasm. He stared at the Bible. "You travelin' alone are ya, Reverend?"

"Waiting for my companions to return." All three men looked none too friendly. Mouths set in thin grim lines, eyes squinted and cold. They wore worn, ragged coats with frayed collars and cuffs from a lot of years, and probably a lot of owners. Their scraggly beards sprouted from under soiled, misshapen hats. It was obvious these fellows did not hail from the upper classes, and if somehow, they ever came into money, it'd be a sure bet it wouldn't for long.

"Must be well-to-do friends you have. Fancy car you're ridin' in." The man doing the talking handed the reins to the man next to him. He, in turn, wrapped them on the brake handle. "We've never seen trappin's like you got here. "Mind if we take a look-see?"

"Well, I don't think . . ."

"They won't mind. We ain't gonna bother nuthin'. Hop off, Frank." The middleman elbowed the man in his left. "You wanna look too, Zeke?" Without waiting for Zeke's reply, he added, "C'mon then."

"Yeah sure, Calvin." Zeke shouted, leaping from the wagon.

"Now, sirs, owners of this train might not like . . ." Venard quickly fronted the coach steps.

"Ah now, preacher, don't you worry none." Calvin said. "Your friends ain't gonna mind us lookin' around. Why don't you stay out here with him, Zeke? Talk to him. Maybe he can learn ya somethin' from that good book o' his'n. C'mon Frank."

"No, wait!" Venard flattened his hand on Calvin's chest.

Zeke whacked the barrel of the Navy Colt on Venard's head. The blow stunned Venard, but he stayed upright. Zeke rolled up Venard's collar into his free hand. "Just hold on there, reverend. I ain't never shot no preacher before, an' I don't want to now, but if'n you ain't givin' me no choice, I'll hav'ta."

Calvin found Luscious seated on the seat. She'd made no attempt at hiding. She thought about escaping out the car's back door and hiding on the other side of the train, but a decision came too late. Now all she could do was wait and see what the men wanted. With the doors closed she couldn't hear the talking outside, and in spite of herself she yelped when the front door burst open.

"Well now, what do we have here?" A crooked smile jumped on Calvin's face. Luscious drew back on the cushion. She tried to get to her feet. Calvin leaped forward and landed on her hard, pinning her against the seat. Calvin pulled her up and swept her arms behind her. He pinned her wrists against the small of her back and then held them there with one hand. He tore at her bodice with the other. It took three hard yanks to rip it open. Cupping her left breast in a brutish grip, he pinched the nipple, pinched it hard.

"Ow!" Luscious tried to buck him off. She swung her head left, away from Calvin's rancid breath, and then back right when Calvin released her breast and grabbed her chin. "Let me go!" The blond hair flew back and forth, sweeping against Calvin's face and beard.

Frank stood by the door and watched. A grin came and went. At first, he enjoyed the scene. The smile faded though when his loins began to stir. Anger darkened his face.

Calvin moved his hand behind and pulled up her dress. Luscious screamed higher, louder, terrified at what was about to happen. He jerked down her bloomers. The lowered waist band tightened her thighs, frustrating Calvin's love-making advances.

It didn't matter. Frank's gun barrel crashed against Calvin's head, putting an end to his ardor. Calvin slumped to the side. Frank shoved him to the floor. Luscious started to rise, grateful for the rescue. It wasn't a rescue. Frank franticly tore at his belt and crotch in an effort to free his rapidly growing manhood. He lost his balance and fell on her, shoving her back on the cushion. As he tried to free his manhood, he used his free hand to tear at the bloomers.

The brief sense of freedom crushed by an attack from the new assailant made Luscious scream, a shrill, frightful screech.

Outside, Venard recovered somewhat from the head blow, heard the scream and leaped for the train. He'd staggered to the step and had a foot on it when Zeke hit him again with the gun. It stunned him, but he fought on. Another blow, and then another, and the train floated away. He fell forward and slid off the step, landing face up. Four more times the pistol barrel whacked him on the forehead. An angry Zeke kicked him. He kicked him and kept kicking.

Zeke kicked until his head got yanked backward and a steel tine was rammed in his mouth. The sai's needle point pierced Zeke's throat. Another hard thrust and the sai dug deeper. The skin bulged out the back of Zeke's neck. Outside Zeke's mouth, a hand jacked the handle up and down, making Zeke's head to nod in rapid agreement. The tine raked against vertebrae. Blood spurted from Zeke's mouth. He choked and coughed, spraying globs of crimson onto the sai and the hand holding it. He coughed again, weaker this time, and then Zeke went limp. The sai came out, and the body fell to the ground.

Stryker pulled the straight razor from his hip pocket and handed it to Tooonug. He stepped over the body and climbed on the train.

As they opened the coach door, Tooonug brushed by Stryker. He leaped behind the kneeling Frank, grabbed a fistful of hair, and yanked hard. He laid the razor against the exposed neck. Tooonug turned to Stryker. "You want talk?"

"No."

Tooonug cut deep, quick, and smooth. He had practice. Lots of it.

"Hey! What the fu. . .?" Frank sprayed "fuck" on Luscious's bare tits. He slumped to the floor, and lay there on his side working his mouth, looking like a cut-throat trout out of water.

Tooonug leaped from the dying man and kneeled, straddling Calvin. He looked at Stryker. Stryker nodded and Tooonug slit his throat as well.

"I think we better dump the bodies out of town," Nicolas said in the doorway. "Are you all right, Mrs. Dhal?"

Luscious repositioned her clothing, covering the sensitive areas before she faced them. She first stared at the two would-be rapists. She shifted her attention to Stryker standing with the sai, and then to Tooonug straddling Calvin with blood dripping from the razor. "God in heaven."

Tooonug wiped the razor on Calvin's coat and handed it to Stryker.

Stryker put the razor in his pocket, and he was wiping off the sai when Venard stumbled through the door. Luscious screamed again.

Venard's face looked a bloody mess. He could barely see out his badly swollen eyes. His face was covered with large purple lumps. Inflated lips and a misshaped nose rounded out the face lift.

Luscious flew off the bench and rushed to him, nearly knocked him over. "Venard! I thought they killed you!" She gently held his injured face. "I thought you . . . I don't know what I thought," she sobbed, hugging him. Pulling back, Luscious studied Venard's face. You need fixin' up. Your face looks awful."

"I feel awful. That man whipped me good. Did they hurt you?" The question really meant, "Did they rape you?"

"No, I'm all right."

As bad as his face hurt, his ribs hurt worse. When she attempted to hug Venard again, lower around the waist, he moaned in pain. "Aaah!"

"What? You hurt? Where? Are you . . . is it . . . bad?" Luscious rattled off questions too fast for Venard to answer, even if his ribs didn't hurt like hell.

"Sit him down and tend to 'im. We're moving out," Stryker growled. "We'll put the bodies in the horse car. Nicolas slid the door open.

Dark clouds had hidden the sun and caused dusk to arrive early. That was a good thing. No shots were fired and Luscious's cries were muffled in the coach. Stryker and Tooonug dragged Zeke to the horse-car. They hauled Calvin and Frank from the coach, one at a time, and loaded them in the horse car as well. Scant light allowed for moving the bodies without drawing attention.

Outside, the wagon and driver had arrived. He'd seen some goings on while still some distance away. After pulling up next to the buggy, he waited on the wagon and remained seated. After things calmed down, he took the clothing and weapons inside the coach. After the last load, he stepped off the train and met the barrel end of Stryker's Peacemaker.

"You're coming with us." Stryker ordered. "Go in and sit down." The driver, being a reasonable man, took a train ride.

The train pulled out of Carson City with Nicolas, and the Dhals seated rear of the coach. Stryker and Tooonug sat in front. Nicolas watched Luscious tend to her husband's wounds for several minutes before scooting up by the wagon driver. The man sat relaxed but quiet, minding his own business. Perhaps thinking if he stayed out of the way, he wouldn't end up in the horse car.

"Those dead men assaulted the lady. When her husband there," Nicolas said, nodding toward Venard, "tried to stop 'em and they beat him up. My two companions saved their lives." Nicolas may have embellished a little, but probably not. "My name's Sanford Nicolas. I'm the lieutenant governor of California." Nicolas sat up straighter. "We're on a special mission up north. Lives are at stake. Time is critical. We can't be delayed. That man seated across from the Indian can be, uh, somewhat unfriendly, best not cross him. But I'd appreciate it if you'd come along and drive a sleigh or wagon. Frankly, I'm not sure what condition you'd be in if he'd left you behind."

The driver glanced at Stryker, who'd pulled the Stetson down over his brow, and then again at Nicolas. "Happy to help."

Stryker dozed. Tooonug remained stoic. He fixed his stare on the man who'd befriended him and didn't move. What thoughts occupied him while he watched Stryker would be difficult to guess. But killing Frank and Calvin at Stryker's bidding provided a clue.

Stryker drifted into a light slumber quickly. It had been a while since he'd slept. Restful sleep seldom came to him. Years in the Army trained him to remain half-awake, with part of his brain still sensitive to external happenings, and ready to wake him. It kept him alive. Other than bullets or shrapnel, sleep deprivation is the most dangerous threat on the battlefield. A soldier has to grab a slice of sleep whenever and wherever he can. But Stryker's resting wasn't free of the nightmares. Like the one about Leigh. Those like it haunted him since her death. Dreams occur prior to deep sleep, or afterward, right before awakening. Stryker never had a deep sleep.

It was a fire-power demonstration that day for indirect artillery fire. Stryker, a civilian, post military, was in charge. Until then, artillery used direct fire. Targets were line-of-sight to gunners, but that also put them line-of-sight to the enemy. In-direct fire changed that, but it required accurate target acquisition and accurate map co-ordinates.

Leigh and her family had been picnicking in a meadow, in a safety zone outside the impact area. However, target co-ordinates were changed, switched by an unscrupulous competitor. Stryker hunted the man down and left him dying, impaled against a wall with a saber in his gut. But once Stryker achieved vengeance, grief was no longer cut by anger. Now what remained would stay with him forever, grief . . . and guilt. He should have double-checked the gun settings.

The artillery shell landed out of the intended impact zone and exploded in the midst of the Enderson family picnic. Only Leigh survived, but just for a few minutes. Long enough for Stryker to ride out and find her. He sat her up, and she said his name before she died. He left her body on the ground. Death ended everything.

In the dream, she wore a white dress. White, like the dress she wore the day of their wedding. But it turned red, bright red, and then black. Her face was covered in blood. Her eyes plead for his help. Then her face faded to black, and she was gone.

His knee. Someone grabbed his knee. He tried to move his leg, shake it loose. He couldn't. "Stryker." They called his name. "Stryker." Louder this time. He jolted awake. Tooonug was holding his knee, shaking it. "You have bad dream."

Shit. They all looked at him. Stryker got to his feet and looked out a window. It was dark outside, and he saw only his reflection. "Let's dump the bodies."

Stryker and Tooonug made their way down the aisle to the rear doorway. Venard's face had been cleaned of blood, but the puffiness made his face look as if it were a balloon. Dried blood, crusted and black, stained his coat. He and Luscious watched Stryker and Tooonug pass without comment.

"Shall I help?" Nicolas offered.

"No," Stryker grunted.

Outside, it was very dark. Heavy clouds blocked out any moonlight, and when he looked skyward, snowflakes flooded his eyes.

Stryker stepped on the coupling, letting go of the platform rail, he lunged forward and grabbed onto the horse car ladder. He worked his way round to the rail car's side, where he used the slats for hand and footholds to reach the loading door. The frigid wind froze his hands, and he fumbled with the latch. It was hard to see, and he could only feel the latch. Letting with numb hands. He finally got it open. He threw himself inside, falling over the dead men. He held his hands under his armpits a moment, then rolled off a body and got to his feet. As he stepped toward the door to look for Tooonug, the Paiute came crashing thru the doorway, sending both men tumbling on the bodies. Neither man thought it was funny. The dead men didn't either. It was too damn cold for Stryker and Tooonug, and Calvin and his buddies were too damn dead. Their bodies had grown stiff, the cold accelerating rigor mortis. And they had frozen together, clinging to each other as pals in death. Stryker and Tooonug pried them apart. They stood the bodies up, the loading door too narrow to roll them off. They simply let each one fall out. After taking a few minutes to warm their hands, Stryker and Tooonug started back to the coach car. Tooonug went first. Stryker closed the loading door and followed. Facing forward on the moving train, the hard-hitting snowflakes stung the eyes, and they had to feel their way to the front of the car. Tooonug stepped on the coupling and grabbed onto the platform rail in a quick, easy movement. Stryker took a little more time.

Venard and Luscious sat slumped against one another in the coach, their eyes shut, attempting sleep. Nicolas watched as Stryker and Tooonug entered, saying nothing when the two men walked past him to the front. The wagon driver scooted to make room for Tooonug. He'd changed seats while the bodies were being dumped, deciding now to sit next with the Paiute, and not by Stryker. They warmed their hands over the small stove before taking their seats on the plush cushions. Stryker sat alone, the way he liked it.

The three frozen bodies provided a nutritious bounty for winter predators struggling to survive, and only a few bare bones, not even resembling those of a man's, were all that remained when the snow melted in the spring.

The Dhals, not able to get comfortable, gave up trying to sleep. Nicolas took the opportunity to tell them, "It's about forty miles north from Reno to Hallelujah Junction. I estimate we're about halfway now. We turn west at the junction."

"Why's it called Hallelujah Junction?" Luscious rubbed her eyes with her knuckles.

"It's not much of a junction, really. North-South tracks meet East-West tracks, and that's about all it is. Emigrants arrived there and saw Beckwourth Pass cutting between higher peaks and yelled hallelujah, is what I hear," Nicolas chuckled.

"Better than holy shit," Stryker growled. He was in a sourer mood than usual, and he was determined to stay awake the rest of the train ride. No more of those embarrassing dreams.

About an hour later the wagon driver got to his feet and moved to sit by Nicolas, maybe to talk, maybe to improve the view by sitting across from Luscious. "Curious, where exactly are we headed, sir?"

"Johnsville," Nicolas replied. The rails run to Mohawk. We travel overland from there, seven miles."

"Driving sleighs," The wagon driver said, staring at the gorgeous girl.

Nicolas noticed and leaned closer. "Three men got their throats cut doing what you're thinking about."

"Names Curt, most call me Cutter." He tore his eyes off Luscious and eyed the mixed-breed.

"And Cutter, that man you're staring at can be a disagreeable fellow. Don't cross him," Nicolas whispered.

"That Injun a friend o' his?" Cutter spoke low and away from Stryker and Tooonug.

"He has no friends. Got the Indian out of prison to come with us."

"In prison? What'd he do?"

"He killed two men."

"Oh." Cutter shifted uncomfortably on the cushion. "Why's he want him along?"

"To kill more." Cutter got under Nicolas's skin.

He whispered to Nicolas, "I drive a sleigh to Johnsville and I'm done, right?"

Nicolas nodded. "I'm gonna see how hard it's comin' down." He pressed his hands against the seat, pushed himself up, and walked out the rear door. Ambient light inside the coach came through the door's glass, reflecting on the falling flakes. Nicolas scrunched his face into a worried frown. He went back inside. "Coming down harder."

"That means trouble?" Venard asked. "Trouble" stumbled through bubbled lips.

"It can get deep in Johnsville–can be deep going up to Johnsville. Better wait in Mohawk til morning. Not much of a town, but they have rooms." Nicolas glanced at Stryker with no response. "Gettin' bogged down in snow during the middle of the night is no fun. Could be life threatening." He got no argument.

The snow hazard dampened conversation. The new problem gave them something else to worry about. Little else was said until the train slowed approaching Hallelujah Junction.

"Coming to Hallelujah Junction," Nicolas said. "We head west now. Go over Beckwourth Pass to Beckwourth, the town, and then we begin a slow gradual climb to timber country. From there we take the Sierra Valley Line on up to Mohawk. It'll be late when we get there." Nicolas rambled on with the proposed route without anyone else paying much attention. They probably thought they'd get there when they got there. Nicolas had more to tell, but he shut it down for lack of interest.

The tracks then ran due west. The Stanford began a steady climb, not steep enough to require curves or switchbacks, but steady. If the occupants could see outside, they'd notice after traveling an hour or so. The bare landscape acquired a few trees. They rolled a little farther, climbed a little more, and trees covered the hills. The rails curved south, dropped lower, and crossed the Feather River. Snow was coming down hard by the time they pulled into the tiny hamlet of Mohawk. End of the line. The rails had been laid for hauling timber, and this was all the lumbermen needed for carrying logs. Besides, getting on up to Johnsville from Mohawk would require a lot of switchbacks over the steep grade. Freight wagons carried supplies the rest of the way to Johnsville and the mines.

The Stanford rolled to a full stop. The door swung open, and the brakeman woke everyone in the coach except Stryker, who was already awake. The sun would come up over the mountains in a few short hours, but the people in Mohawk and its new arrivals might not notice it until well into the next day. Mornings on snowy days like this one crept into town shrouded in dark trappings.

Nicolas struggled awake and pasted his face against the window. Light from a hanging lantern on a building told him they'd arrived in some kind of settlement. "Mohawk?" he asked the brakeman.

"Yep."

Nicolas lingered at the window. The lantern light silhouetted the flakes. They looked as big as silver dollars.

The brakeman spun back to the door. That was it for him. He left. He and the other rail men were likely relieved to be rid of their passengers, especially Stryker and Tooonug.

When Nicolas turned away from the window, Stryker was digging in the coats and equipment. He pulled out two heavy canvas dusters, one medium, and one extra-large. He threw the medium coat to Tooonug. He laid the other coat behind him and continued rummaging through goods bought in Carson City. He handed the Winchester and a box of shells to Tooonug, along with a hunting knife. He set aside a box of the .44-40 shells for himself.

Nicolas slipped from the cushions to join Stryker. Stryker, having pulled out what he needed, tried on the duster. Tooonug fitted the knife in his belt. He awkwardly donned the duster over his deerskin shirt and pants. A fitted coat with sleeves required a different technique than throwing on a buffalo robe. He finally got it on and looked very prideful. Nicolas separated the other three coats for the Dhals and himself. Cutter was SOL on coats. He'd have to make do with the jacket he'd worn in Carson City.

They all got off the train wearing new clothing, except for Cutter, who wore his old jacket. The long dusters dragged in the snow, anyway. The brakeman slid the door to the horse car open and laid down the ramp. It lay flat from the car to the snow. Stryker, with Cutter and Toooonug stepping behind him, tramped along the tracks to the ramp. Nicolas hesitated and then followed. The roan was brought out first. Stryker led it off the ramp and down off the deeper snow. Nicolas did the same with his mare. They waited by the train while the brakeman and Cutter brought out the last two horses. The brakeman handed his reins to Tooonug.

"Cutter," Nicolas said. "There's a sack in the middle stall. Would you go back and grab it please?" He turned to Stryker. "Bring the horses on up ahead," Nicolas shouted. He waved his arm forward for Stryker to lead the horses between the engine and the station platform buried under deep snow. "Got a livery back of the station, we'll stall 'em inside."

The brakeman hustled up to the engine and climbed aboard. In a few minutes, the Stanford began backing out of Mohawk. Evidently, the engineer chose not to wait around for deeper snow, or maybe he wanted to avoid whatever mischief his passengers got into.

Upon stabling the horses, Nicolas gathered everyone and led them through three feet of fresh snow to a wooden two-story boarding house. There were ten-plus wooden structures lining the street section on the Graeagle-Johnsville Road. Most were one story. These comprised wood clapboard houses, two saloons, a barber shop, a hardware store, a post office, and a few other commercial enterprises. Some buildings off Main Street stood two stories. They walked past a tavern where Nicolas had downed more than a few hot rums. It sat in front of the night's lodging. There were more places to spend a night, however Nicolas preferred the boarding house where he'd become friendly with the woman who owned it. But no lights shone from the windows. Nicolas pounded on the entry door for several minutes and got no response. Stryker fired a shot with the Peacemaker, and a few minutes later the door cracked open.

"Mrs. Robinson," Nicolas cheerfully greeted the cherubic face at the door. "My friends and I need lodging for the night."

"Nicolas! What are you doing here this time of night? And it's going on morning, early morning, damn you."

"We just need rooms for a little while to rest and wait for the storm to pass. It's cold dear, may we please come in?" Nicolas asked, with a little edginess' of his own.

The door swung open. Mrs. Robinson showed them through a small vestibule to a larger room serving as the lobby. She stepped behind the desk counter. After lighting two lamps, she turned to face the guests. Mrs. Robinson was a stout woman. Certainly not fat, but she could pass for an Army Sergeant. She had the stern face for it. Grimly set mouth, angular cheekbones, and a permanent frown, all she lacked was a soldier's uniform. "How many ya got wit' ya?"

Nicolas approached the desk. "We'll need three . . ." Nicolas swiveled his upper body and glanced behind him. He saw Stryker's glare. "Four, we'll need four rooms, and you'll bill the State, of course." Nicolas added billing information with trepidation. He probably knew what was coming.

"The State, my big ass," Mrs. Robinson huffed. "The last time you come here, you said the State would pay. They paid, if you want to call it that. I got the money six months later and . . . and they only gave me half of what they owed me—said that was the going rate for rooms like mine." She wagged an angry finger. Nicolas backed up two full steps. "Unless you pay me up front, you and your friends can just march your State asses out of . . ."

Stryker came around the Dhals and stepped to the counter. "How much for the rooms?"

"Uh, they're a dollar-fifty a night for each room." Mrs. Robinson noticed Stryker's own fierce features and lowered her voice. "But I can include . . ." Before she could finish, Stryker slapped a ten-dollar gold piece on the countertop. He banged it on the counter fast and loud. She thought he'd fired a gun. "Eeee-yeahhh—breakfast!" Her eyes lit up when she saw the money. "It includes breakfast. Yes siree, breakfast included."

Mrs. Robinson turned her back again and took four room keys from numbered hooks on a board. "Follow me. You'll be on the second floor."

The Dhals, of course, were given a room for themselves. Cutter and Tooonug would share another.

"Cutter put the bag in my room first. Thank you." Nicolas said.

Cutter opened his mouth as if to protest about the room arrangements, but evidently decided against it. He shut his mouth and followed along, carrying the sack. Stryker and Nicolas each received their own rooms. Cutter deposited the bag in Nicolas's room and walked out without a word. He rushed down the hall to make sure there were at least two beds in his room before Mrs. Robinson went back downstairs.

Stryker walked in his room, allowed Mrs. Robinson to light a table lamp and leave prior to his looking out the window. From what he could see, it hadn't let up. He threw his hat on the table, sat on one of the two beds, and took off his boots. After unstrapping the gun belt, he pulled the Peacemaker from its holster and laid the belt beside the bed. He put the Colt under the pillow. He stretched out on the bed with his clothes on.

Three hours later, he woke. He withdrew the Colt from under the pillow, slid it back in the holster, and strapped on the belt. He peaked out the window. It was still dark outside. He saw dull mornings in San Francisco, and he'd been on the trail in rain and snowstorms, but he'd never seen it this dark past dawn. His inner sense told him the sun had risen. One sure couldn't tell it. The snow was coming down even thicker than before. The clouds acted as a blanket, and no light at all peeked through. *Shit, a damn blizzard.*

Stryker met Tooonug and Cutter emerging from their room.

"Don't know Mister Stryker," Cutter said. "If it don't let up, I can't see how we go out in it, much less have them horses pull wagons up that hill. Even with snowshoes on 'em, they'll sink up to their bellies in this soft stuff."

"Snowshoes, on horses," Stryker said, as they walked down the hall, feeling their way toward the stairwell. The two wall lanterns had burned out. A feint glow from the first floor crept up the stairway, and it threw off enough light to guide them to the stairs.

"They're metal plates on horse's hooves," Cutter offered, walking behind Stryker. Tooonug strode silently behind him. "About a foot square, I reckon," he threw in. Actually, they weren't square. They were slightly longer than wide. "Keeps 'em from sinking too deep. Debatable on how well they work in snow like this, 'specially heading uphill."

"They work fine," Nicolas bellowed behind them. He had come out into the hall. "Used them up here before. The brutes seem to learn how to angle 'em in the snow." Nicolas waddled up behind and then slowed when he bumped into Tooonug.

Stryker started down the stairs. The enticing aroma of fried bacon wafted up to greet him and he quickened his steps. Cutter kept up with him. Not Tooonug, he took his time. Nicolas also caught a whiff of breakfast and followed impatiently behind the Paiute.

Their noses guided them to the dining room. It sat opposite the lobby, across from the entryway. Not very large, it contained six round tables. Four straight-back chairs sat around each table. The dining room seemed crowded even when empty. Tables and chairs sat too close together. Four tables would have worked better. Evidently, Mrs. Robinson figured the guests would rather eat bunched together than wait. Two windows set in the raw wooden paneling, one window provided a view out front, and the other one looked out at the next building eight feet away. Neither window had curtains. Blue and white checkered tablecloths covered the tables. The chair backs almost touched, and Stryker waded through them on his way to his preferred seat–back to the wall, facing the door. Cutter trailed behind and scraped out a chair to join him. Tooonug took the next table. Stryker noticed the Paiute carried the hunting knife. He wore it stuffed in the leather belt, near his left hip. Nicolas had a little more trouble squeezing through the chairs and shortened his journey. He capitulated and sat at the first table. That worked out fine because the Dhals appeared in the dining room, and they joined him.

Mrs. Robinson heard the chairs scraping, and she soon emerged from the kitchen with three plates of pancakes, two on one arm, and one on the other. Each plate was stacked with four pancakes and two strips of bacon. She crashed through the chairs, banging them into tables, and served Stryker first. Wading back between the tables, she gave the Dhals the two remaining plates, and returned to the kitchen. A little while later, she came out and dropped plates in front of Nicolas, Cutter, and Tooonug. After another trip, she came back with the coffeepot, and once again Mrs. Robinson served Stryker first.

About half-way through breakfast, other guests filtered in. First a man and a woman arrived, and then a lone male traveler old enough to have been in the war, and another man, athletic looking maybe in his late twenties. Three more men came in together. The last three could have been drivers for the wagons and or sleighs, or maybe they were miners. A brawny six-foot bearded man led the other two men, also with beards, to a table. Stryker kept an eye on them.

Cutter sat at Stryker's table He sat by Stryker rather than the Paiute and kept his mouth stuffed with pancakes.

Stryker watched Tooonug eating alone. The Paiute held the pancake in his hands and ate it like a sandwich. The fork lay unused on the table. Tooonug had a deeply tanned flat face and black obsidian eyes like most of his race, but Stryker thought the most striking feature was the man's mouth. It was just a grim line. Stryker had never seen it any other way. Tooonug must have had it chiseled on his face in the womb. He sat studying the Indian, and thought Tooonug wore the same expression when happy, sad, or angry, except Tooonug was never happy–or sad. He probably had that straight line for a mouth whether he was killing, shitting, or fucking. Once he'd had a wife. He told Stryker the Utes stole her and tortured her until she managed to impale herself on a broken tree limb. Perhaps that had something to do with his and Stryker's unlikely kinship. Both had dead wives who died trag-ically. Only Stryker didn't figure Tooonug grieved. Grief fell on Tooonug like rain on granite. All it did was make the stone wet. And he couldn't imagine Tooonug having nightmares to haunt his nights. He probably didn't dream anything at all; his mind shut down while asleep. Once before, the two men had almost fought. It was over the roan. Tooonug knew Stryker had watched him fight with a knife during a Sun Dance celebration. That night when Tooonug demanded the roan for his own, Stryker stood his ground, brandishing the sai. Tooonug, a pragmatic man, wisely backed off. But weeks later they met again. They struck an uneasy bargain when Stryker gifted Tooonug horses owned by men he and Tooonug had just killed. Now that Stryker had plucked his ass out of prison, Tooonug was indebted for life. But Stryker wouldn't have rescued him if he weren't needed. Stryker was a pragmatic man, too.

The three miners sat at the table next to Tooonug. They looked amused at how he ate the pancakes. Two of them were anyway. The brawny miner seated between the snickering men smirks, wore a scowl. Unamused, he failed to find humor in an Indian holding a pancake in his hands, munching on it like he would a sandwich. Miffed their pancakes had yet to be served, and that was bad enough. Now they had to sit and watch a damn Indian who didn't know how to eat one. The men huddled together. They talked in low voices.

The brawny fellow called out, "Hey, Injun. Don't you know how to eat a pancake? You use a fork, like this." He held up a fork and made like he stabbed one on an imaginary plate. He pretended to eat from the fork. "See?"

"Maybe he don't hear too good, Krug" The miner to the left of him said.

Tooonug ignored him. He kept eating the pancake sandwich.

Krug scraped back his chair and got to his feet. He walked around his table and pushed through a couple of empty chairs to stand in front of Tooonug. The other two miners leaned back in their seats, trying mightily to keep from laughing outright.

"We're hungry too, Krug," one miner chortled. The pair traded punches on each other's shoulders.

"Here, let me show ya." Krug raised his fork, held it as if to poke a sausage, and stabbed a pancake. He didn't get it to his mouth.

Tooonug seized Krug's wrist and yanked the miner across the table. Tooonug pulled the knife. Held the blade pointed down and slashed both Krug's cheeks. The action happened so fast, Krugs buddies failed to see it. At first Krug thought he got slapped. Then his mouth filled with blood.

Stryker laid the fork next to his plate and drew the Peacemaker. He placed it on top of the table, pointing it at the miners. Picking up the fork, he got back to his pancakes.

Blood gushed from Krug's cheeks. He lurched backward and fell against the table behind him. His two friends remained unaware of his wounds, even after he sprawled on their table. It wasn't until Krug turned his head toward them; that they realized his face had been sliced open. Both cheeks flapped open. Krug's teeth seemed to be floating in a sea of blood. Krug saw the look of horror on their faces and he vomited.

"What the fuck happened to you, Krug?" One miner yelled.

"Good Lord! You're bleedin' like hell!"

Both men jumped up, banging their chairs against tables behind them. Krug worked up another frothy hurl.

Krug tried to talk in between the heaves, but the words were washed away in a crimson flash flood.

"Here's your hotcakes," Mrs. Robinson announced. She'd come out of the kitchen earlier holding three plates.

The miners, including Krug, stared at the woman who seemed impervious to the bloodshed. Finally, one of them (not Krug) said, "What?"

"You boys look a mess. Why don't you go clean up before breakfast?"

"Ma'am, that fu–Gol-durned Injun just cut Krug!"

"Yes, I see that. He's gonna need stitchin'. He was askin' for it. An' there's a fellow behind me with a gun who might be taking his side."

Krug used both hands on his bearded cheeks to press the flaps together. "Aahhh, can ya sew'm?"

"Go to the kitchen." Mrs. Robinson ordered. "You two go with him." She feigned a smile and added, "I'll be in there in a minute to stitch 'im back together. Go on, now. More pancakes in there. You can eat while your friend here gets that mouth sewed up." She delivered the pancakes she held to Nicolas and the Dhals.

"A moment please, Mrs. Robinson," Nicolas entreated, as she turned to go. "Have you heard about the kidnappings and murders in Johnsville?" He put his elbows on the table.

"Of course," she said.

"Know anything about 'em?"

Venard and Luscious ignored the food as well.

"Big mystery. First it was a boy or two and some girls. Then some turned up dead–two girls, a preacher, now a deacon. Don't make a lot of sense." Mrs. Robinson set her hands on her hips. "Is that why you're here, Sanford?" She scrunched her eyebrows and canted her head. "If that's right, you need help. You ain't no lawman."

"I brought those two." Nicolas hooked a thumb at Stryker and Tooonug. Stryker was sipping his coffee. Tooonug munched on another pancake.

Mrs. Robinson studied the two men and nodded as if she understood. "I see."

"The militia is on its way. Be here in a few days, depending on the weather. Storm could delay 'em. Meantime they'll look into it."

She turned back to Nicolas. "They might be enough."

"Mrs. Robinson, you probably saved those miner's lives," Venard said.

She paused a moment and said, "I better go tend to 'em." She turned to leave.

"Mrs. Robinson, thank you for what you did, and for tending to the injured man. You might tell 'em why they're up here," Venard said, and then he added, "Mrs. Robinson, Jesus loves you more than you will know."

She gave Venard a funny look and headed for the kitchen.

"Excuse me." Another breakfast guest said. He sat alone at the table next to the Dhals and Nicolas.

Nicolas responded for the table. "Yes?"

"I hear you're going to Johnsville." The man, a slim fellow with blond hair and a short beard, cast a quick glance at Stryker. He came back to Nicolas. "I'm headed that way myself, for the races–snowshoe races. I'm entered." He spoke with a Scandinavian accent.

"Ah, the ski races!" Nicolas exclaimed. "They call the long boards, snow-shoes and they ride 'em down hills, fast, really fast. They're skis, actually. People in this part of the country call 'em snow-shoes, not skis."

"Ski races, yes, I'm in them, won last year," The racer nonchalantly said. "I was wondering if I may impose on you for a ride to Johnsville?"

"If we can get ourselves there, you're welcome to come along with us."

The Dhals offered friendly smiles. Stryker remained impassive. Tooonug belched.

"That would be most appreciated, sir. Have you arrangements? Not on foot, I presume."

"We're to meet my man here in Mohawk. Jenkins is his name. He's supposed to have wagons or sleighs. Sleighs, I guess now with the snow."

"Normally, I snow-shoe up there from Mohawk. I get off the train and go up. It's only seven miles. But someone stole the straps off my boards. I have my suspicions. I've won the last three years. Took two days for the man at the livery to make new ones. I coulda' made myself, but nobody would sell me the leather. Finally got 'em on the snow-shoes and now this storm hit." The European talked fast and with his accent he was hard to understand.

"Uh, all right." Nicolas failed to follow everything, but he responded to what he thought he heard. "That's fine. I'm Nicolas. This is Mister and Mrs. Dhal." He pointed across the room. "Stryker, Cutter, and Tooonug."

"What's your name?" Luscious asked.

"Dag, I'm from Denmark." Dag was strikingly handsome.

Luscious smiled and said, "We're glad to meet you, Dag. My husband's name is Venard. I'm Luscious." The alluring name was lost on the Dane, so she went on. "And this man is Sanford Nicolas, Lieutenant Governor of California." That was lost on Dag too. "Those other men Cutter, Stryker, and the Indian Tooonug will all be going up together."

Nicolas sat back and watched as Luscious made the introductions, preferring not to interrupt. When she'd finished, he said, "You should know, young man. Riding with us may mean you'll be subjecting your-self to trouble, and we might run into it. Are you prepared for that? Sure you want to accompany us?"

"Even if it clears, I rather ride up. Don't like to work my legs the day before the races. The main race, the one I compete in, is tomorrow."

If Dag can ski as fast as he talks, he should easily win," Nicolas mused to himself. "Dag, when we get to Johnsville, you'll get to Johnsville." Nicolas said it with a bit of irritation, suggesting Dag should give his tongue a rest and just accept the ride. Luscious showing an interest in the man kinda irked him as well.

"Tomorrow! That's Christmas! They have the races on Christmas Day?" Luscious exclaimed. She seemed a little too excited for Nicolas.

"Yes, starting about noon. You should see . . ." Dag saw the look on Nicolas's face and stopped.

"Oh, how fun! We'll have to watch!" Luscious cried. She turned to Venard, lowered her voice, and demanded, "We have to, please, Venard."

Venard forced a smile and nodded.

"It sounds so exciting!"

"Yes, dear, it does." Venard lacked the same exuberance. He and Nicolas exchanged knowing glances. Having the cherubic, harmless Nicolas flirt with his wife was one thing. The young, handsome, and athletic Norseman was another matter.

For his part, though, the young skier seemed naively unaware he had stirred a heart in one and misgivings in two. He appeared thor-oughly focused on the races, tall athletic body and all.

"You know," Luscious began softly. "Each of you has a different calling. I don't know about the Indian, so I won't talk about him, but you four live a life that you all seem made for. Funny how it works out." She cocked her head and spoke even lower. "You Dag, an athlete. Fits you," she said to the Dane. "And you, Mister Nicolas, a politician, all about laws and such. I don't know a lot of what you do, but . . ."

"That's what I do, dear," Nicolas offered.

"Venerd, you spread the word of God. You preach and you comfort people." Luscious squeezed his hand and let it go. "And him . . ." she pointed at Stryker, holding her hand close to her stomach as if to conceal the gesture. "He kills."

The kitchen door flew open. The two miners who'd been with Krug came out. Hats in hands, they waded through tables and chairs, and stopped at the table where Nicolas and the Dhals sat.

"Mister Nicolas?" The taller of the two men, asked.

"Yes," Nicolas replied. He looked for weapons but didn't see any.

Stryker squared around. His hand dropped to the butt of the Colt.

"You be needin' a ride up to Johnsville?" The shorter miner squeezed up next to the tall one.

"That's right." Nicolas looked puzzled. "We're waiting here to meet the man to take us, should be here shortly."

"We've been told to take you, me and Doug. My name's Evan. Krug too, but he ain't gonna make it now."

"Told you, who told you? Mrs. Robinson? We already have arrangements." Nicolas grew more suspicious.

"Jenkins."

"Jenkins sent you?" Nicolas asked incredulously.

"Yeah, didn't know we wuz to take more than one. So, we wuz waitin' here for a man by his self. Figured he ain't showed up yet. Only feller here by his self is him, (pointing to Dag) and he don't fit the description Mister Jenkins give us. You fit, but you with them." Evan nodded at the Dhals. "Them ones in the corner didn't look right neither." "So we didn't think you's who we supposed to meet." I guess we messed up, more ways than one, I reckon. Now we only got two drivers for three sleighs. Krugs willin', but he ain't fit for calling out to them horses. His mouth's pretty sore and 'em horses ain't gonna under-stand him." Evan, looking solemn, rotated his hat nervously.

Nicolas hesitated and then burst out laughing. "Ha, ha, ha, well, we've got another man for the third sleigh."

"Then sir, we'll be takin' three sleighs." Evan stopped rotating his hat.

"Good, three sleighs. You and Doug each take a sleigh, and Cutter over there will drive the third. I'll ride with you, Stryker too, he can be up front with you. Your man, Doug, will carry the Dhals and Dag. Cutter will bring up the last Sleigh with Tooonug. The horses shouldn't have any trouble understanding him." Nicolas relieved there wasn't going to be more trouble, and he'd found his drivers. He sat back and had another laugh. "Stryker, did you hear?" Nicolas shouted. "We've got our drivers. You good with them?"

"Cutter, get Krug's coat." Stryker got up from the table.

Cutter went to the kitchen and came out carrying the coat in his arms. "It was lying on a chair. Krug was getting sewed up, and I just took it. I'll bring it back though," Cutter said to Evan.

"When do we leave?" Nicolas gazed out the window. Sunlight seeped through the cloud cover, and he saw snowflakes outside the glass. "It's still snowing hard."

"A couple of drivers came down this morning before sunup. They broke trail with a ten-horse team." Evan was in his element now. "When we have these heavy snows, we like to break trail coming downhill if'n we can. It's still snowing hard, but the clouds are starting to loosen a bit. Maybe before long it'll let up some. Anyway, we . . ."

"A ten-horse team?" Cutter joined them. "How in the world ya handle ten of 'em?"

Evan turned to Cutter. He allowed a wry smile. Now he could really impress. Even their own man didn't know how to control a team of horses. The railroad coming through reduced the need for a big team to break trail hauling freight. Only a few teamsters knew how to run a large team these days.

"In the first place, we don't use all horses. We use mules. Only use horses for wheelers. And we use a jerk line up here. We connect 'em all to the wheeler the driver rides on. He don't sit in the wagon or sleigh. And he just pulls right or left on the jerk line to guide 'em. Them mules are pretty God-damned smart and . . ." He glanced at Luscious. Did a quick bow. "Excuse me ma-am." Then he went on without waiting for a comment from her. "Them mules'll even jump the chain to keep it tight for to take up slack on a turn. You can't teach a fu . . . uh, a dang horse that." Evan paused a few seconds and beamed. He continued and quickly added, "We'll have a team lead us up the hill. They'll be dragging a looped chain behind the sleigh to level what we broke through earlier this mornin.' Won't need ten though, maybe six'll do."

"So, when do we leave?" Nicolas asked again.

"Should be ready to leave in an hour, or maybe a little after that. We'll get the teams out, get 'em harnessed to the sleighs and be out front of the hotel then. Look for us. C'mon Doug." Evan slapped Doug's shoulder. "Let's go to work."

"I better go with them Mister Nicolas," Cutter said. "I need a refresher on working a jerk line."

"Go ahead," Nicolas said. "Dag, since you're riding with us. You can help out with a few chores."

"Certainly, sir." Dag may have finally picked up on Nicolas being an important man.

"Good. Go upstairs to my room, second floor, third door on the right, and bring the large sack downstairs."

Dag, seemed surprised at the request, hesitated, waiting to see if Nicolas was actually serious.

"Soon son, before we leave." Nicolas wasn't smiling.

Dag said nothing. He jumped to his feet and headed up the stairs to the second floor.

"You'll put the bag in the last sleigh, the one Cutter drives with Tooonug," Nicolas reminded Dag.

Dag stopped and turned.

"Put your snow-shoes or skies, as you call 'em, in that sleigh too," Nicolas added somewhat curtly. A worried frown crossed his face, as if he wished he hadn't put Dag with the Dhals. Damn. Too late.

"What's in the sack?" Stryker had strolled over to the Nicolas table, holding his cup.

Nicolas, surprised he hadn't sensed anyone behind, swung himself about in nascent anger. It quickly subsided when he faced the mixed-breed. "Oh, I bring up a few things for the kids."

"Presents? You bring the children presents?" Luscious exclaimed. "How sweet of you!"

"Oh, it's nothing really. The children don't get many store-bought toys up here. I try to pick out a few things I can carry. I'd say it's as much fun for me as it is for them," Nicolas chuckled.

"Do you know all the children?" Venard asked.

"Well, no. I have to make a list." Nicolas seemed to be getting a little embarrassed. "They're real young, you know. Most of the parents are from Europe. They had a hard life there. Had a hard time getting here. And now they have a hard life in Johnstown. It's not much, and I only bring 'em toys once a year."

"It's so wonderful of you. Saintly, I'd say." Luscious gushed.

"You do that for the Chinaman kids?" Venard wanted to know.

"I didn't use to, but I saw the disappointment in their faces and now I bring them a little something too. Really, it's nothing." Nicolas squirmed. He looked up at Stryker, who sipped his coffee, showing no interest. And Tooonug sat across the dining room staring at him, stone faced. "You make me feel a little foolish." Nicolas kinda smiled, looking down at his feet. "I'm a grown man. The Mrs. used to tell me I'm just an old fool."

"Oh no, don't feel that way," Luscious said.

"Thank you," Nicolas said. He sat up and gazed around at the men's faces. He got nothing from their blank stares. Just the woman, a pretty woman, and that made him feel even more embarrassed.

"Uh, well." Luscious changed the topic. "Stryker, are you a religious man?"

"I'm gonna check on my horse." Stryker set the cup on the table and walked from the dining room. A moment later they heard the front door open and shut.

Tooonug followed across the floor between the chairs, hardly touching them, slipping stealthily between, as one would expect an Indian would do.

Nicolas whispered at Venard. "Jesus."

"I know. I didn't hear him either."

"A pair, those two," Nicolas said.

"Why's he like that?" Luscious asked no one in particular.

"He's Indian," Venard replied.

"No, Stryker. Why is he the way he is?"

"On the train, remember? He was sleeping and moaning something awful. Never heard such a tortured wail from a man. Whatever's in his past must be pretty bad."

"The war?" Venard suggested.

"Could be. Although, Hearst told me he had a wife who . . ."

"He had a wife? My God, what woman in her right mind would marry . . .?" Luscious cried out.

Dag came in, carrying the sack over his shoulder and his fourteen-foot snowshoes. He stopped to listen too.

". . . died in a bad accident," Nicolas finished. "Anyway, I wouldn't ask him about it. No telling what he would do. A man so bothered is not a man you want to dig into. Leave him be. Let's just hope he can do something for us in Johnsville."

"Let's hope," Luscious said, her voice drifting off.

CHAPTER SEVEN

No sign of the sleighs outside. Stryker started off toward the stable with Tooonug following. The snow was deep, four or five feet in places, even more where the wind built drifts on the leeward side of buildings. But the snow was letting up; flakes were falling smaller, and not as many. They heard the sleigh drivers before they saw them. Shouts to the horses and mules–mostly mules–mingled with tack rattles, animal snorts, and bell jingles, broke the silence of a snowy morning. Stryker rounded the livery stable where he saw the animals lined up by twos in front of four sleighs. An enclosed roof extension of the livery provided room for sleigh teams to be harnessed under cover. A sliding door allowed the teams to be brought out from inside the livery. Two teams had already been harnessed and waited in line at the harness shed. A snow-packed incline acted as a ramp from under the shed where there was no snow to the street level track. Once winter set in, packed tracks in the streets were used for sleighs in town. Keeping them groomed was easier than constantly clearing snow down to the ground for wagons.

Stryker had not seen the lead drivers before and thought they might be the ones who came down from Johnsville that morning. A heavy chain lay in the snow behind their sleigh, a freighter which looked more like a traditional wagon on skids. The other three sleighs had a raised bench seat in front with two padded lower seats behind, facing each other. These travel sleighs carried six. Evan was strapping snowshoes on four mules and two horses for the second sleigh. Doug and Cutter, along with two other men, who probably worked in the livery, pulled on straps and buckles, testing harnesses on the two sleighs under the shed. Stryker figured the livery hands must have already harnessed the teams before Evan, Doug, and Cutter got to the livery. Doug pulled Cutter aside and led him to the lead sleigh, where they climbed onto its seat. Stryker stood by Evan as he fastened on the metal plates and watched as Doug gave Cutter a jerk line lesson. Then Stryker stomped around back of Evan's rig and side-steeped down the ramp. He still hadn't swapped the slick Hyer boots for ones with rugged soles. He went inside the livery and found the roan tied to a post, waiting to be brought out. Doug came in the livery and grabbed a belly band off the wall.

"My horse needs those plates on him," Stryker said, as Doug brushed past him.

It took a moment before Doug realized it was a question. "Puttin' him behind a sleigh, are ya?" Doug asked.

"Yes."

"Be a good idea, I reckon. We ain't got the trail packed too good. He could step in a deep hole. Get drug forward. Snap a leg."

"I need shoes for him," Stryker said.

"What sleigh is he going behind?"

"Second, Evan's. I'm riding with him."

"Soon as I replace a worn-out belly band . . ." Doug held up the replacement to show Stryker. "I'll put 'em on for ya. He had 'em on before?"

"No."

"Better walk him a bit. Let him get used to 'em."

Doug left the stable and came back with the broken strap. He hung it on a nail and pulled four hoof plates from a barrel by the door.

Stryker stood next to the roan and watched Doug strap the snowshoes onto its hooves.

"That ought to do it," Doug said, straightening up. "Take him for a little walk before ya tie him behind the sleigh." Doug tipped his hat and walked out the livery. He wrapped a gloved hand around the lead mule's head stall. Leaning forward with his arm outstretched behind to pull, he led the mule and the rest of the sleigh team up the ramp. Doug didn't wait for a "thank you" which wasn't coming, anyway.

Cutter's sleigh was still under the shed, and with a team still needing snowshoes. Doug dug his heels in the snow ramp and quick-stepped down to ground level. He entered the livery and emerged with an arm full of plates. "Grab more outta the barrel, Cutter." Doug dropped the plates by the lead mules.

Stryker figured it'd take another fifteen minutes to finish strapping on the plates. He turned to Tooonug who'd been shadowing him and said, "You ride this one."

Tooonug climbed on the seat. He sat stiffly with crossed arms, looking stoical.

"Watch behind," Stryker said.

Tooonug kept his shoulders forward and nodded to Stryker.

Stryker retraced his steps to the hotel. He found Nicolas, the Dhals, and Dag all seated at one table. Mrs. Robinson was there too. She was standing by their table and telling them about the prior year's snow, when Stryker walked in the dining room. Four more tables were occupied with diners now, all men except an old woman who sat by herself in the corner. They were all listening to Mrs. Robinson. A waitress Stryker hadn't seen earlier rushed in from the kitchen, carrying plates of food. Much younger and more attractive than Mrs. Robinson–although that was a low bar–she moved among the tables with the same efficiency as the older woman, maybe more so, since her hips weren't as wide. She dropped off plates piled with pancakes and/or biscuits and sausage to the men. She gave a saucer with a single biscuit to the old woman seated alone.

"Mrs. Robinson," Nicolas whispered. "Can you give the woman a little more?"

"Who's payin', you or the state?"

"He's paying," Stryker said.

Nicolas sharply turned to Stryker. "Why yes, I am." Nicolas stumbled out the words and fumbled in his pocket. He produced two bits and carefully placed the coin in Mrs. Robinson's outstretched hand.

"Sleighs will be outside in a few minutes. Get your stuff and get out there," Stryker said.

The lead sleigh was pulling up when Nicolas opened the front door for the Dhals. He let them pass and immediately followed them, cutting in front of Dag. Stryker intended to leave last anyway, but Mrs. Robinson called to him.

"Mister, if I hear any word on who's doin' the killin' up there in Johnsville, I'll send word to the Sherriff. People talk. Sometimes I listen, and sometimes I learn things."

Stryker tipped his Stetson.

But as he turned to leave, Mrs. Robinson added, "When you catch 'em, make 'em sorry for what they done. Make 'em real sorry." Her face turned dark. "Killing them girls like they done, they don't deserve a quick trip to hell. If I catched 'em, I'd make the passing as painful as I could. You do that too, now. Don't let them do-gooders up there, turn the other cheek. You make the bastards pay here on earth before you turn 'em over to the devil. I ain't trustin' no afterlife, and I sure as hell ain't trustin' them church people neither. You look like a man who can put a lot o' hurtin' on a fella, you and that Indian you got with ya. Make 'em have regrets–big ones. Now you go. Find them and kill 'em. Kill 'em all like I said."

She'd talked fast–and she'd talked hard.

Stryker's pale gray eyes locked with the woman's. "I'll pass your good wishes on to Tooonug."

"God be with you." Mrs. Robinson said.

Stryker opened the front door and walked out to the sleighs. He ignored her bidding to have the deity ride with him. Guns would do.

All four sleighs had pulled up outside and drivers stood by them to assist passengers.

"Here Miss," Doug took her case, a purple flowered, oblong piece with a shoulder strap, and set it on the ground. He extended a hand to Luscious. "Let me help you climb in." Luscious took hold of Doug's hand. "Thank you so much," she said in a voice befitting angels. Doug held onto her hand and wrapped an arm around her waist to help the beautiful woman into the sleigh. He jumped into the sleigh and gently spread a blanket over her. He didn't offer help to Venard or Dag. His legs were probably too wobbly, anyway.

Doug hopped out, carried the case to the last sleigh, and set it inside. Venard hadn't offered his bag to Doug. Maybe he carried a bible or something important in it. Regardless, he kept it with him, stuffed under an arm as he climbed in. He placed the bag between his feet.

Stryker climbed in the second sleigh with the Winchester he'd gotten off the roan and sat on the driver's bench. However, Nicolas needed a push on his rear from Evan. Evan took his place next to the mixed-breed and Nicolas settled on the rear cushion, with a blanket on his legs.

Cutter and Tooonug climbed on the driver's bench of the last sleigh. They climbed on from opposite sides and failed to exchange pleasantries.

"Shouldn't take more'n a couple hours to Johnstown," Evan called over his shoulder to Nicolas. He noticed Stryker staring at him. "Johnsville, they changed the name a while back. Don't know why."

The two drivers in the lead sleigh faced rearward, waiting patiently. Now, satisfied everyone was ready, they turned forward. With a "Heeya" and a snap of the jerk line, they set off up the hill to Johnsville. The three sleighs behind started out in order. These sleighs used regular reins instead of a jerk line.

The wagon road to Johnsville began up a long grade and then curved left after about a mile. Talk was held to a minimum, each rider satisfied with his own thoughts as they glided along, the silence broken only by the jingling bells. In fact, the sleighs glided so silently, drivers long ago started using the bells to keep from running into each other.

Evergreen trees of cedar, spruce, fir, and pine lined both sides of the road, their boughs weighed down by snow from the recent storm. Longer branches sank lower, and you couldn't see their tips buried in the fluffy powder. The trees, bearing their heavy burden; nevertheless, they appeared regally majestic, standing tall against the sky that had now grown blue. In a remarkable change of weather, but not one uncommon, the system moved out and only a few isolated clouds, white and puffy, dotted the sky. The pines crowded alongside the road as if they were soldiers guarding the route. The dazzling beauty of the fresh snow glistened in the sun. If it weren't for the trip's grim reason, the travelers might have ridden along in a mood of merriment.

Only the bells and an occasional animal snort interrupted the idyllic sleigh ride. An hour and half seemed to fly by, and they were not far from Johnsville, so peaceful was the ride.

But then they rounded a curve and saw a man's head balanced on a post. The lead sleigh came to a stop, and its two drivers stared at the ghoulish ornament. It hadn't been there long. Fresh blood dripped down the post.

Stryker, puzzled as to why they'd stopped, followed their gaze and saw the decapitated head. He raised the .44-40 to his shoulder and fired. The large caliber bullet smacked its forehead, blasting the head off the post. "Take off." Stryker ordered.

"No! Wait!" One of the lead drivers yelled. He turned back to Stryker. "That was Carl!"

"Take off, dammit!" Stryker jacked a fresh round and fired a bullet between the two drivers.

"Carl?" Nicolas asked behind Stryker. He hadn't seen the head. "Butcher? You shot Deacon Butcher? Why?"

"Get down!" Stryker shouted, firing into the trees.

The lead sleigh bolted forward as another shot rang out, this time from the trees. The driver on the right took the bullet in his throat. A second shot hit Evan in the chest. Stryker held the Winchester in his right hand and grabbed the reins. He managed to work the lever again and sent a second round toward the woods. The lead sleigh paused, but then sped up as the other driver took the jerk line.

Stryker fired again, this time directly to his right. Hampered by holding the reins, he couldn't get the rounds out fast enough. But by now Tooonug had fired two sleighs back. Both hands free, Tooonug poured lead into the trees.

Doug had the good sense to speed his sleigh forward as the Dhals and Dag dove to the floor.

Cutter hunched down beside Tooonug, who continued firing and yelled as he snapped the reins.

No more shots came from the trees. The lead driver kept the team running hard for another half mile. By then, the animals were giving out, and he had to slow. He brought the sleigh to a full stop on a downhill grade about a mile from the bridge over Jamison Creek.

The driver shot in the throat, rolled back in the sleigh and flooded its floor with blood. He died choking in it.

Stryker pulled Evan upright and saw the death mask on his face. He figured that was close enough and shoved Evan off the sleigh. Evan landed face down in the snow. The two sleighs behind slid by without stopping.

"Mike's dead." The lead driver shouted, standing in inch deep blood. "What happened to Evan?"

"That man kicked him off." Doug shouted back, bringing up his sleigh. Venard helped Luscious from the floor where she'd huddled by Dag. He pulled her next to him on the seat.

"He dead?" The driver asked.

"Dead weight," Stryker replied.

Doug leaped from the sleigh and ran back to turn over Evan's body. "Yeah, he's dead."

"Get in your sleigh." Stryker ordered.

"We can't just leave him here," Doug protested.

"Come back for him, How much farther to Johnsville?"

"Not far. We cross that bridge and then up around a bend." The driver said, shaking his head. He faced to the front and snapped the jerk line.

"You knew it was an ambush? How?" Nicolas asked. He moved to the cushion behind Stryker and hunkered down.

"The head was still draining blood. Figured whoever put it there was nearby."

"My Lord." Nicolas settled lower and peeked out over the sleigh, searching in the trees.

The road wound down to Jamison Creek and the bridge stretching over it. The creek itself was but a thin canal. Snow covering the banks had nearly closed together over the fast-running stream, leaving only its middle visible under the snow. On the top of the bridge, two boys appearing to be in their mid-teens shoveled snow.

"Hi, y'all," one boy called out.

The driver in front halted his sleigh at the edge of the bridge. "Boy, is Sheriff Bandy in town? We need him."

"I guess so," the kid replied.

The second boy stopped shoveling.

"We'd ride up with ya, but we gotta clear the bridge so it don't bust down. One already did farther up the creek," said the first.

"That's all right. If he's in town, we'll find him." The driver snapped the line.

The boys saw the driver's body, but they stood far enough away to miss seeing the massive pool of blood on the floor. They saw Nicolas in the second sleigh as it passed them.

"Hey, it's Mister Nicolas!" The second shoveler cried out, breaking into a run, high stepping in the snow, after the sleigh.

The first boy who'd gone back to his shoveling, threw down his shovel and took off after the sleigh too, yelling "Hey! Mister Nicolas! Wait!"

Stryker pulled back on the reins.

But when the boys caught up with it, Nicolas threw up his hands, palms out. "Boys, I'm sorry. We've had two men killed. I'll have to visit with you later."

"You mean he's dead?" One of the boys asked, pointing at the lead sleigh. They drew away from Nicolas, looking up at Stryker.

Nicolas saw them eye Stryker. "No, not him, he didn't do it. He's with me." The lead sleigh hadn't stopped. "Let's catch up, Stryker,"

Nicolas said, conjuring up a weak smile. He looked back at the boys until they rounded a curve at the top of the grade.

The boys spied the large sack in the last sleigh sliding past, but their excitement had drained. Ole Nick brought death with him this year.

Stryker took his time closing the distance to the sleigh in front, allowing Doug and Cutter behind him to keep up. By the time he'd caught the lead sleigh, they'd gone up the steepest section of grade from the creek. The road made a sharp right turn ahead. They made the turn and the Plumas-Eureka Mine complex; at the bottom, Gold Hill came into view. It was much larger than Stryker expected.

Nicolas noticed him studying it. "It's something, huh? It's the largest employer in the Plumas County, over 350 men. All of it owned by the British, the Sierra Buttes Mine Company. You know much about gold mining, Stryker?"

"No."

"They have to process 2.5 tons of ore to get one ounce of gold. This mill does 50,000 tons a year. That big building up the hill there," Nicolas tapped Stryker's shoulder and pointed at a large, multi-story wooden building with a slanted roof. "That's Mohawk Mill That's where they crush the ore, sixty stamps, the most of any mine around here. The mine shafts are higher up the mountain, at least sixty miles of tunnels. Bring the ore down to the mill in those ore buckets. See 'em hanging from the cable up there? The snow-shoe racers get in the buckets and ride them up to the top of Gold Hill. They jump out and come down the hill on boards like Dag has. It may well be the first lift for skiers." Nicolas pointed farther up the mountain beyond the mill, but Stryker no longer looked at the mill, or mountain. He was scanning ahead and behind. Nicolas mistook his scanning for curiosity on the surrounding structures. "Oh, yes, those are boarding houses for the men. And . . ." Nicolas finally noticed Stryker had lost interest in the mill. "If they mined lead, he'd be interested," Nicolas mumbled to himself.

They entered Johnsville proper. Again, Stryker was surprised. Johnsville appeared much different from other mining towns he'd seen.

Europeans made up the population. Welsh, Scots, Germans, Italians, Greeks, and Serbs lived in the town and worked the mine. Rather than rough-hewn logs cobbled together to build single story dwellings, Johnsville housing was constructed with planed lumber. Multi-story homes and commercial buildings had white and green clapboard painted sidings. A fire had nearly destroyed the town in 1882, but it was re-built and now sported two hotels, a jail at the Sheriff's office, three general stores, two meat markets, several blacksmith shops, more or less five saloons–depending on the season–a barber shop, a library, a school, a post office, and a well-attended church on Church Street. All told, there were over a hundred buildings of different sizes and shapes. Arastra Street, the longest one in town, ran perpendicular to Main and circled east around to intersect Main again farther north. There were also a few shorter lanes as well; Church, School, and Pine Streets east of Main and Eureka Street west of Main.

"Stop at the Sheriff's office," Stryker called to the driver ahead." The four sleighs lined themselves in front of a single-story building with a sign out front which read, "Mortimer Bandy- Sheriff." Bells ringing from the horses' head tossing brought Sheriff Bandy to the door.

"Sanford, you old Pol, what you . . .?" The Sheriff surveyed the sleighs as he greeted Nicolas, starting with the first one, habit for a seasoned lawman. His eyes locked on the slumped form and he stopped. "Dead?" He asked, trudging over to inspect the body.

"We got ambushed, Sheriff." The driver spun all the way around on the seat. Shot him and another man we left on the trail."

"Why d'ya leave him?" Bandy asked, lifting the dead driver's chin.

"I kicked him off," Stryker said.

"And who are you, other than the lieutenant governor's driver?" The sheriff let the dead driver's head drop.

"Senator Hearst sent him up here with me, Mort." Nicolas cut in quickly to head off a confrontation between Bandy and Stryker. The Sheriff was a longtime friend. Chances were he would come out second in a clash with Stryker. Sheriff Bandy at over six feet was a powerfully built man, muscular with big knotty forearms, square jaw, and so on. He had sent many a man to the floor with his big and heavily scarred knuckles. If he weren't sheriff, he could've easily been the town bully. But Nicolas had heard about Stryker's run-ins. None of those men survived. He'd seen his quickness with gun and razor, and whatever the hell that forked weapon was. And another thing Nicolas learned about the mixed-breed–he fought to kill. No one got a second chance.

"The senator?" Bandy nodded knowingly. I mighta knowed he'd send somebody, anyway. I mean, only the Governor can send troops."

"Troops are on the way, too, Mort," Nicolas said. Might be a few more days. They have to organize, and we came through a bad storm. Could hold 'em up.

"George and me. We go back a ways. That's why I sent the telegram to him. I don't know the Governor," the Sheriff said.

"Well Mort, you coulda ask the Gov. . ." Nicolas started to say.

"Yeah, I know," Bandy said. "But I figured you'd have trouble talking him into it. Johnsville ain't got a lot o' votes, like them big towns on the coast. George owes me. I called in a favor. I'll tell you about it sometime."

"Hearst can tell him," Nicolas admitted. "Mort, forget all that. We got more problems."

"Yeah hell, there's more gone missing. Two more girls, four more boys in the last three days. The Butcher kid been gone, I don't know how long. We thought he went to Reno. Now his father, too. The town's disappearing."

"Carl Butcher," Nicolas allowed.

"Deacon at the church," Bandy added.

"Found him, Mort. His head was on a post about a mile and half back. We got ambushed there."

"God almighty! What the fuck is going on here?" The sheriff's eyes scanned the last two sleighs as he cursed. They stopped on the third sleigh. "Who's she?"

"New preacher's wife." Nicolas knew who he meant without looking. "Venard Dhal, and his wife, Luscious."

Venard raised an arm in a half-hearted wave.

Bandy tried his absolute best not to burst out with a laugh. After all, the kidnappings and killings were a serious business. He leaned closer to Nicolas. "Did you say her name was Luscious?"

"Yes," Nicolas whispered.

"You all have to come inside and make a report on what happened!" The Sheriff said in a loud and authoritative voice. He glanced at the last sleigh prior to opening the office door, presumably checking for another angel. He gave a little grunt and pushed the door open. Inside, the Sheriff positioned two chairs directly in front of his desk.

The law office had a desk and a small table on which rested a full plate of sausage, biscuits, and gravy. Two chairs sat off to the side of the desk. A gun rack holding a twelve-gauge and a Winchester hung on the wall behind the desk. A bunk looking recently used lay behind the desk. A rear door led to the jail cells in back. The one window in the office faced the street and had no curtains. It did have shutters which could be closed to cover the glass. A bookshelf on a side wall held books and papers. On the top shelf was a coffee pot. The walls were all painted pale green, and the floor was bare except for a foot rug by the door. A U.S. flag and the California state flag hung on two separate polls in the far corner.

Nicolas held the door open for Luscious to enter first. Bandy gently took her forearm and guided her to one of the chairs. He gave her a warm smile after she sat. She returned a polite one. Mortimer with his square jaw and fit physique did fancy himself a ladies' man. He was married. His wife, Gertrude, taught school and sat on the school board. A small woman, but she was a tough keg of nails. The first time Bandy came home drunk, banging against the walls in the hall, Gertrude met him halfway and landed a straight hard right, knocking the yet-to- be sheriff on his ass. He woke up the next morning wondering how he got a black eye. He'd never come home drunk again. Mortimer and Gertrude had no children. Seeing the two together though, one could hardly imagine they had sex, kind of like they were your parents. Nevertheless, Bandy never actually committed adultery either. He only flirted, a big flirt, but so far that was all.

Nicolas and Venard performed a silly duel by deciding who would take the vacant chair next to Luscious. The issue was settled by the Sheriff. "Please be seated, Governor." He left out "Lieutenant", probably on purpose, adding official justification for giving the chair to Nicolas; after all, he was a man of importance. And it would be somewhat awkward ogling a beautiful woman sitting next to her husband.

Venard, Dag, Doug, Cutter, and the driver formed a loose semicircle, standing to the rear of Nicolas and Luscious. Venard stood behind his wife. Bandy furrowed his brow.

Tooonug remained outside, tending the horses and mules. The implacable Paiute would take no questions. He'd give no answers.

Stryker sauntered over to the coffeepot. He laid a palm on its side, then grabbed a mug to fill the cup. Steam rose as he poured, and the coffee smelled rich and strong.

The Sheriff watched Stryker get the coffee. He opened his mouth and shut it and again said nothing. Stryker's looks did not invite rebuke. Finally, Bandy asked, "Would anyone else like coffee?"

"That would be nice," Luscious said sweetly. No one else wanted any.

"I'll get it," Dag volunteered. He stepped back and practically leaped toward the pot.

Stryker leaned against the wall, out of Dag's way, sipping his coffee.

Bandy waited until Luscious got her cup and tasted it before he said, "Tell me as much as you remember about the ambush. Wait; first tell me your names." He pulled pencil and paper from the drawer. He wrote down their names, only asking Luscious to spell hers. "Now what happened out there?"

Nicolas took lead and recounted the ambush. When he finished, Doug and the lead driver, whose name they finally learned to be Zeke, made a few more comments.

Bandy asked where they'd be staying in town.

"Tell us what's been going on here, Sheriff," Stryker said, leaning against the wall.

Frowning, Bandy swung his attention to Stryker. The frown took its time slinking away as he spoke. "The Butcher boy left town about a month ago. We figured he went to Reno, got drunk and found a whore . . . uh, a lady friend and stayed." He smiled at Luscious. "Didn't think nothun' of it. He's done it before. Then, about ten days ago, one of the O'Brien girls disappeared. Three more in town turned up missing a couple days later. We found two of 'em charred. We still don't know which ones they are. And four boys are now gone, left or taken over the last several days." The frown dissipated.

"Other towns missing kids," Stryker asked in a statement.

"Don't know." Bandy sounded frustrated, probably thinking he should have checked.

"Ask around, Reno too."

"Well, I . . ."

"Telegraph them. Do it now." Stryker sat the cup on the table. "I want to know how many are in the cult." He started for the door. "Let's go find a room, Nicolas."

Nicolas turned his attention from Stryker to the sheriff. Bandy got to his feet. His teeth clinched, his face reddened–he looked ready to explode. Nicolas shrugged his shoulders as if to apologize for Stryker's rudeness. But when he saw Bandy's hand drift toward his gun, Nicolas's eyes flashed large and he frantically shook his head. "What hotel or rooming house would you suggest, Mort?"

Bandy's face grew redder. He held back a huge breath and tightened his jaw.

Stryker walked out the door.

"He killed two men on the way here. That Indian, two more," Nicolas warned. "One made the mistake of drawing on him. The other three, well, they tried to assault the lady."

"He's awfully fast, and you'd be five. I wouldn't like that." Luscious chose her words well.

Bandy released his breath with a loud huff. "The Johnsville Hotel is probably near full of the racers comin' to town. You might try the Mountain House, or..." he paused for a split second. "The Odd Fellows Lodge on the second floor of the schoolhouse has beds to let, if you can't find a room. A woman named Gertrude is who to see there."

"Your wife, Mort?" Nicolas asked.

"Yeah, you remember?"

"I thought she taught." Nicolas rose from his chair. He *bent* down and offered a hand to Luscious.

"She still does. They let women in the Order several years back. Gertrude's a member, two years now. Works, uh, teaches downstairs, rents beds upstairs." Bandy ran around the desk and pulled out Mrs. Dhal's chair. Venard stood back and allowed the two men to embarrass themselves. Nicolas extended a forearm to Luscious. The sheriff stepped lively to the door and held it open.

"Thank you so much." Luscious floated a smile to the sheriff.

"Sometime, tell me about that man, Sanford," Bandy said, stepping aside for Nicolas and Luscious. He continued staring after the gorgeous woman, unwittingly holding the door open for Venard and the three drivers.

Stryker saw Tooonug tended the horses. He stepped between the teams and out to the street where it lay packed save for ridges pushed up against the boardwalks. He looked up Main Street for a hotel. Snowshoe racers, men and women, carrying their long boards, some, especially the stouter types, hauling them on shoulders, walked hurriedly on the streets. Others moved easily about with the boards strapped to the feet. They used a long wooden pole to propel themselves or to slow down. Stryker had never seen anything like it. It was as if he'd ridden into a strange and foreign country where the mode of transportation was on these long wooden boards, snow-shoes they called them. Agile and effortless, they made it look easy. Right away he figured if he were to find and stop–kill probably–the cult members, he might have to do it on those damn boards. Somehow, he'd have to make the cult come to him or surprise them somewhere.

"Oh, look at them on those long boards!" exclaimed Luscious. She'd come up beside Stryker. Together they marveled at the people skiing by on the boards.

"Some men racing tomorrow are in uniform," Nicolas said, joining them. "See how tight they wear their trousers? The hats on those fellows walking together carrying the boards, those are their team hats. And the women, girls I reckon, they wear dresses, but you can kinda tell if they race. All the racers have the long snowshoes. If they don't race, they'll mostly have shorter boards. They use the longer ones to go fast. They put a special–they call it dope–on the bottoms of the boards to go faster down the hill, and boy, do they! Some go ninety miles an hour!" Nicolas smiled to himself. "I used to race. I used to go fast."

"Gotta have good dope. Dope is king!" Dag came up to stand between them, not actually between Luscious and Nicolas, but behind and between, and Luscious turned to smile at him. "I'm fast now," he said.

"I want to watch you!" Luscious squealed, tugging on his arm. Her eyes spoke even louder, sparkling as they did with excitement and admiration.

Venard, standing by a sleigh, noticed his wife's enthrallment with the Dane's sporting prowess, or his accent, or maybe just the man. Venard said nothing.

"That looks like a hotel, The Johnsville, I reckon." Stryker said, and he started off down the street to it.

"Bring my bag!" Nicolas shouted, breaking into a fast waddle to catch up with Stryker. The street was icy and slick from the boards, and Stryker slipped several times, awkwardly catching his balance. At first, he side-stepped the snowshoers gliding past him, then he realized they were like acrobats on the boards and skilled enough not to run into him. They were jovial, laughing and shouting good-naturedly. It seemed a pity to plug one with the .44. So, he didn't reach for the Peacemaker. Instead, he simply watched and admired the frivolity. *How does one get to that level of happiness?* After nearly busting his ass a number of times, he reached the hotel steps and got out of their way.

Doug and Zeke peeled off after a few steps and returned to the sleighs. Cutter noticed the two drivers turning back and stopped. He stood in the middle of the street with his arms folded across his chest, warming his hands in his armpits. It appeared he was debating to bring the sleigh with the bag or just bring the bag. Groups of snow-shoers parted like creek water around a smooth rock to avoid hitting him. Eventually, he made up his mind and shuffled off after the two drivers. "Gimme his bag!"

Nicolas paused on the hotel steps, watched Cutter turn back, and shrugged his shoulders as if to acknowledge Cutter's decision. The Dhals and Dag brushed by, following Stryker through the door. "Well, all right, Cutter, don't fall with it," Nicolas mumbled, and he entered the hotel.

"Only got one room left," The hotel clerk, a short, thin wisp of a man, said behind the counter. He talked like he looked, crisp and fast. His lower lip quivered a little. Maybe he wasn't sure.

Stryker was about to change the fellow's mind when Nicolas interrupted him. "Let them have it, Stryker." He stepped aside, opening the space between himself and Stryker, and directed an outstretched arm with an open palm to Venard. "Meet your new preacher and his lovely wife–they've come a long way," Nicolas said to the clerk.

"C'mon you two." Nicolas bade the Dhal's, his smile a cheerful one.

Venard and Luscious, acting a little unsure, stepped up to the counter.

"You're the new preacher?" the diminutive clerk asked.

"Yes," Venard said with a preacher's smile. Men of the cloth smile as if "My son" is understood.

"Then you'll want the clergy house. It's by the church on Church Street, that way and around the corner." The clerk pointed a shaky finger at the wall with mail slots behind him.

"Mrs. Dhal, here's your case," Doug huffed, placing her purple luggage bag by her feet. He'd run, slipped, lost his balance, fallen to his knees, performed all kinds of acrobatic feats except drop the bag, and he was out of breath.

Luscious melted him with a radiant smile. "Thank you."

Dag picked up the bag.

Doug scowled at the Dane, spun curtly, and headed out the door.

"Will you be taking the room, sir?" The clerk rotated the register book.

"Yes," Nicolas replied.

"Mountain House," Stryker growled. Nicolas pretended not to notice Stryker's irritation.

"I'm sorry, sir, no vacancies there either," the clerk advised. "You might try The Odd Fellows accommodations. It's on the second floor above the school. Follow them to the church house. You'll run into School Street off of Church Street there."

Stryker considered tending to the roan first, but he figured the horse would be cared for by Tooonug with the rest of the animals. He'd get a room first.

The Dhals walked out the hotel. Dag followed with the purple case.

Stryker laid the Winchester on his shoulder and went out behind them. Walking on Main Street, now harder and icier than ever, put the mixed-breed in an even nastier mood than usual. And usual was pretty damn nasty. *Fucking open bay beds. Better than nothing. Shit, nothing is a low bar.*

The small party of four turned right on Main Street and continued on it for roughly five hundred feet to Church Street. Again, they turned right, and not too far down the street was the church with a nativity scene next to the building. A person or persons had taken a lot of time putting it together. A shack with a roof and three walls was built to house the manger scene. The front lay for the display. There were mannequins, one of Mary, who sat on a bale of straw watching over a baby–also plastic and in a cradle–and another of Joseph, who stood next to Mary. A live donkey and two sheep were tied to a stake in a set of three wooden rails used as a make-believe stall. The live actors munched on straw strewn on the ground. A fake star made of shiny foil hung suspended on fishing line, which ran from the shack's roof to high on the church. The mannequins must have come from a big city with stores having display windows, Stryker figured. It was a carefully constructed birth scene of Jesus and his parents.

Venard and Luscious came to a stop by the manger scene. They stood without speaking, as if silently remembering why Venard had come to Johnsville.

Nearby, School Street ran North and perpendicular from Church Street. Stryker hadn't felt the same biblical calling as Venard. He headed for the next street.

The Dhals said their goodbye's to Dag. Luscious held his hand a second too long. Once again, Venard noticed. Stryker turned onto School Street. The hell with silly salutations. The streets away from Main weren't as packed, not as slippery either. Not much, but busting his ass might get the next son-of-bitch who crossed him shot. Again, that was a low bar–always is.

The first floor of the schoolhouse was empty of children. It was the Christmas holiday until January first. Classroom desks clustered four separate sections, a group by each of the four walls. Different grades, Stryker guessed. Crayons and scattered crude drawings on papers lay on one group of desks, the earlier grades. He couldn't tell if the grades went around the room clockwise or counterclockwise. In one corner were several boxes, and Stryker could see pine boughs in one of them.

Gertrude came down the stairs upon hearing the door open and close. She looked as tough as nails, all right. What Gertrude lacked in stature, being five feet tall, weighing ninety-eight pounds, was made up with one hundred percent grit. You could see it in her face. A face that could make shit leap from a bedpan and run out of the house. Fugly wasn't even close. Her skin was lighter, of course, but it was if someone had traced Tooonug's grim facial features on plain paper and stuck it on Gertrude's face. This was one hard piece of ass, Stryker mused.

"What you two want? Schools out." Gertrude talked with her teeth ground together.

I wouldn't want that woman's mouth anywhere near my cock. "Bed for the night." Stryker said, meaning one for him.

"You two together?" Gertrude asked. She acted none too pleased at the prospect.

"You can have him," Stryker snarled. "You married to Bandy." Stryker asked in a statement.

"That's right."

"He sent me."

"Come upstairs. I'll show you what there is. Ain't much, but it's better'n outside."

Stryker and Dag followed Gertrude up the stairs. She stomped up the steps as if each one held grapes to be crushed. The room was about the same size as the classroom downstairs. An elevated stage stood at the far end. There were ten circular tables with straight-back chairs clustered around each one. No windows on the sides, but both ends had a window, and they allowed in enough light to keep from bumping into tables.

"I'll take that bunk," Stryker said, pointing with a wave of his hand. The bunk was in a corner with another, presumably set together for man and wife, and they were the only beds in the room. Stryker put a boot on the other bunk and shoved it into a table. "That's for him. Take it downstairs."

Stryker gave Gertrude seven dollars, the amount she'd asked for a week's stay. She'd also provide breakfast in addition to the beds, she told them.

"C'mon pretty boy," the woman told Dag. "Grab the end of that bed. We'll put in my office. I need help setting up for tonight. You're gonna help me. Payment for the bed."

Dag went to the end of the bunk. One couldn't tell if he did it for the free bed or a stern woman's order. Dag probably didn't know himself.

Stryker jogged down the stairs ahead of Dag and Gertrude carrying the bunk. Outside, a few clouds began to wander in, nothing threatening. As Stryker made his way back to Main Street, he passed more people on their snowshoes. All of them seemed to not only tolerate the snow, but these people acted as if they actually enjoyed it. *Some town, this Johnsville.*

Passing the church, he saw a girl putting candles in the windows, not lit, but maybe they would be when it got dark. The gaiety on Main Street still abounded, and Stryker saw other signs of the Christmas season. Four boys pulled two snow sleds, two to a sled. Ropes were tied to the front of the sleds with the other ends fastened around sturdy four-foot branches. Two boys pushed against a bar, pulling a sled behind them. On each sled lay a freshly cut blue-tip spruce tree. A dog, probably belonging to one of the boys, ran around the sleds, wagging his tail and yapping at the trees. Pine wreaths hung on doors, and around the door frames they'd placed garland with red ribbons on them. A group of three boys and three girls carrying boxes and packages walked toward him, singing a song he'd never heard before. It had the words snow and sleigh and bells in it. They sang very loud, and they laughed while they sang. He stopped to watch them pass.

Stryker was seeing something he'd never seen before–really seen, that is. Joy and merriment. He felt as if he were behind a large glass window with his nose crushed against it, watching what was happening on the other side. For a brief instant–a very brief instant–, he thought about what it would have been like to be there with Leigh. A terrible ache shuddered through him. He pulled his nose from the glass and walked on.

"Stryker!" Nicolas burst out the front door of the Johnsville Hotel as Stryker was walking by. Nicolas hurried across the stoop to the street, nearly falling as his foot slipped. He remained upright though, as upright as his round body could be. "Hey, Stryker! Wait a minute." He slowed now that Stryker turned to wait. "I talked to that clerk in there about the murders and he said something, might help." Nicolas paused and looked at Main Street's mirthful activity as he tried to catch his breath. "You'd never think there'd been any killings. Look at 'em. They sure seem awfully happy, don't they?"

"He said what."

"The girls, he said there's more that's gone missin' that's been killed. Boys too. And none of the boys gone missin' have turned up dead like the two girls. The girls they found dead were new here, hadn't been in town more'n a couple weeks. What'cha make of that?" Nicolas took a really deep breath.

"Sheriff knows more'n he's telling." Stryker started up Main. He walked a few steps and then angled across the street toward the Sheriff's office.

"I done tolt ya what I know," Bandy said. "Yeah, I sent telegrams to towns from here to Reno, even Truckee. Ain't heard back nothin' yet."

"Total number missing," asked Stryker.

"I don't know," the Sheriff said, part frustration, part whine. "There's a few missing, but this time of year with school out, they've been known to sneak a trip down to Mohawk, or even on to Truckee. Older ones do it. Them kids was born on snowshoes."

"Truckee." Stryker said.

"Get down there less'n a day. They sometimes take the train back, if they have too much fun. It's uphill coming back." Bandy allowed a half smile—one of those knowing, sarcastic smiles, by a smart ass.

"I need snowshoes," Stryker said.

"You ain't gonna learn them long ones quick enough," Bandy advised. "Takes a full season for that. Get the short round web ones at the store." He pointed in the general direction.

Stryker left the Sheriff's office. He went farther up the street and saw the sleighs parked by the stables. They appeared small and useless without the horses. He started walking toward them.

Tooonug, who'd been waiting outside, sitting in the last sleigh, saw Stryker coming toward the stables. He lightly leaped to the ground. The Paiute moved like a mountain cat no matter what he did.

"We need snowshoes," Stryker said. The two men had never extended greetings to each other and didn't now. "Short webbed ones."

Tooonug acknowledged the need for snowshoes with a dip of his head.

"The roan," said Stryker. "He's cared for."

"Yes."

"Come with me." Stryker started careful steps, returning to the middle of town. Tooonug had no trouble keeping up. The Paiute spent half his life outdoors in snow. The other half he spent outdoors on bare ground. Tooonug managed to keep his footing without much difficulty, and the proud brave walked beside Stryker, not behind him. Stryker had no problem with that.

Johnsville General Store fronted Main Street near the middle of the village. Main Street was simply a half-mile section of the Graeagle-Johnsville Road which ran through town. In that section, two hardware stores competed for business, Johnsville General being one of them. Stryker had used the teardrop snowshoes before, traveling through the Dakotas in the Army. He and Tooonug strapped them on outside. Although unwieldy, they maintained good purchase in the snow. These snowshoes were no match for the swiftness of the longboards, but they would be especially handy in deep snow. There would be no pursuit and catch on these shoes, no pursuit and kill on them either.

CHAPTER EIGHT

It drizzled all day in San Francisco. It made for a wet and miserable day for shoppers making their last-minute purchases on Christmas Eve. Stores had yet to make a significant appearance on the streets surrounding Union Square. Union Square, named after Union victories in the Civil War, had been leveled by steam paddies and not much was on the roughly 2.6 acres of space bordered by Geary, Powell, Post, and Stockton Streets. Occasional statues had come and gone. Graveled diagonal footpaths crisscrossed the square. There were areas of grass, a few trees such as Dracaena palms and Island pines, and scattered non-native plants. Most of the large spaces around the square were taken up by churches, huge stone edifices with towering spires. The corner of Powell and Geary held Calvary Presbyterian Church. Trinity Episcopal Church sat on Post and Powell, and Stockton and Geary had First Unitarian Church. Paradoxically, close by on what was then known as Morton Street, which ran east from Stockton Street, was a row of whore houses, San Francisco's first red-light district. Perhaps they needed all the churches to provide redemption for the abundant carnal sinning taking place a few feet away.

Nevertheless, a few stores had begun to appear around Union Square, sprouting up like new vegetation between the churches.

Already an area in San Francisco attracting shoppers who sought the convenience of multiple stores in one location, the square was littered with people carrying packages. Two of the shoppers carrying boxes wrapped with brown paper and string were Morgan Bickford and Myrna Angle. They walked the diagonal gravel path toward Geary Street where the two women rented flats. Morgan lived on the second floor and used the two-room apartment to stay while in San Francisco, that is, when not staying at the Palace Hotel as a guest of Senator Hearst, or when Stryker came to town. Myrna kept a studio on the third floor. She'd become a widow three months earlier. Stan, her late husband, had been shot relieving himself in an alley. The thieves even took his pocket watch. It happened in the early hours one morning, after an evening of regaling over his favorite horse buggy tales, in an Irish pub called "O'Malley's."

"If it's going to be gloomy and dark like this, why can't it be snowing," Myrna said, in an attempt to talk about something else besides the rain running down the back of her neck. With arms loaded with packages, neither woman held an umbrella.

"I didn't know it snowed here," Morgan said.

"Well, it doesn't, not that I'm aware of."

"You ladies need help with them boxes?" The particularly filthy vagrant asked sarcastically. He'd stepped from behind one of the pine trees. The man was bone thin with a face blackened from standing over warming barrels. His cheeks were hollow, eyes sunken, and teeth brownish. Morgan and Myrna both knew he had no intention of helping carry their packages. Instead, they figured he planned to run off and sell the stuff as fast as he could and then go to the nearest opium den. The square had also become a favorite resting place for opium addicts who frequented the dens in nearby Chinatown. No longer able to find work or hold a job, even if lucky enough to get one, the wretched souls stole to get money for opium. Sanctimonious church goers and do-gooders on Nob Hill called them unfortunate homeless, but most of the unfortunates were either rum-soaked drunks or opium addicts. A select few were indeed unfortunate and could then be pointed out as casualties of *heartless capitalism*. Some wealthy on the hill needed to assuage their guilt, especially if they weren't the ones who actually earned the money causing all the guilt. If they got other people to donate money for the homeless, they felt better.

"Keep walking," Morgan whispered.

"That's right. Just keep walking," The vagrant yelled. He pulled out his penis and finished what he was doing behind the pine. "Hey, I got somethin' here for ya!" He pushed hard and launched a tight, powerful stream. The piss blasted out a tiny circular clearing in the pebbles. The remaining urine in his bladder splattered into the little lake. There the piss stream made an even louder noise. He smiled broadly.

Morgan kept a flat on Geary Street, renting a two-bedroom accommodation on the third floor of a house which had a sign outside that read "Rooms for rent." Often, Senator Hearst provided a room at the Palace Hotel, and she'd spend a night or more there. The visits with the senator weren't for physical motives, though. Instead, Hearst simply liked to hear the woman discuss philosophy and current events. Morgan possessed an exceptionally keen mind, and often their talks would extend deep into the evening.

She stayed on Geary Street when she wasn't at the Palace, or off on a mining assignment for Hearst. Morgan, a mining engineer, was second only to the senator's expertise in the mines. She'd learned her craft in classrooms. He'd learned his digging in the shafts. The second bedroom was for her son, Lucas, when he came to visit. Lucas, still a teenager, struck out on his own after his father was killed in Bickford. He'd met Stryker there. It was less than cordial.

Morgan and Myrna said short goodbyes. Arms ached. Clothes wet. They climbed the stairs to their rooms.

Myrna lived in a single room flat one floor above Morgan's. She and Stan had done okay as actors, and they made shrewd investments. Hearst had helped with that. That year the couple bought The Stage Door Theatre on Geary Street, a small neighborhood playhouse. It was a dream come true. They'd wanted to stay nearby. But maybe now she'd sell it.

Myrna had bought Christmas presents for the employees, not much, one gift per person. Juggling her load, she managed to get a key in the lock and shove the door open with her foot. Leaving it open, she crossed the room and dropped her packages on the kitchen table. Staring at them, she wondered if those were the last Christmas gifts she would buy for the troupe. She missed Stan. Overall, he was a good man. He took good care of her and remained devoted. Sometimes he got on her nerves like when he acted too bossy, but who knows, maybe she rattled his nerves as well. Anyway, he was gone, and she was on her own. "I could use a gin and tonic," she said out loud to his ghost.

"Pour me one too." The vagrant stood in the doorway. He looked nervously around the room. No other door. No other room. No other person. He walked with put-on confidence across the floor. "Remember me? In the square," he said. At first, the tramp tried to be cordial. Who knows, maybe it'd work. Maybe she'd like him. He flashed a crooked grin, showing off his brown teeth.

In the confines of the apartment, he smelled even worse. "Get out!" Myrna backed against the table.

The brown ivory disappeared. "Money! Give it to me!" He snarled.

"No," Myrna said, her voice now slightly above a whisper.

"If you don't, I'll kill you. Rape you first. But I'll surely kill you. Give me the damn money!"

"It's in my purse." Myrna turned and picked it up off the table. She dug her hand inside, faced him with her hand in the purse, and fired.

The bullet from the Derringer blasted through the cloth purse and hit him in the gut.

"Did you just shoot me?" The vagrant furrowed his brow, and his mouth hung open with disbelief. He put his hand on his stomach. It came away bloody. "I can't believe you shot me!"

Myrna pulled the gun out of the purse and fired the double-barreled Derringer again. The second bullet hit his chest.

The would-be rapist and killer staggered backward. He turned. But his knees weakened, and he sagged to the floor. Lying on his side, he propped himself up on one elbow. "I need a doctor."

"Most likely." Myrna opened a cabinet door and withdrew a small cardboard box. She scooted out a chair and sat. She opened the box and put two more bullets in the little gun.

"It hurts bad," he groaned.

Myrna stood and opened another cabinet. First, she took out the gin bottle and sat it on the table, and then she brought out a bottle of tonic. Still holding the Derringer, she grabbed a glass from the same cabinet and poured two fingers of gin and one of tonic. She raised the glass, saluted it at the man on the floor, and took a drink.

"Aren't you gonna help me?" The tramp tried to sit up but fell back on his elbow. He was breathing hard now. "Just gonna sit there?"

"Yep."

"Do nothing'?" Pink spittle drooled out his mouth.

"Gonna watch you die. I'm sure, when you took that first drug; you never thought you'd end up this way. But like a fool, you hopped on the drug train, and here you are, dying on my floor. You do anything before?"

"Lawyer."

"Hmmm."

"Jesus, lady." He groaned, holding his stomach. It must have hurt more than his chest.

"He told me to shoot you. What's your name?"

"Tim."

"Yep, Jesus said, 'Myrna shoot Tim.'"

"Please, I can't do anything now. Show some fu . . . some pity, please."

"I go outside. I see dog poop on the ground. I don't pity it. Why would you pity shit? Now that's how I see you–shit. You or someone like you killed my Stan a few months ago. Shit is something to walk around, stay away from. But you shit, you came into my home and I shot your ass. Now I'm gonna enjoy watching you die." She got up, walked around Tim, and closed the door. Going back to her seat, she said, "I've got things to put away so hurry up."

"Ohhh, it hurts!"

"Aw hell." Myrna rose again and picked up a medium-sized pot off the stove. It felt empty. She walked over to the dying man and swung the pot as hard as she could. It struck him full in the face, and she went back to her chair.

So, Tim bled from a busted nose and a smashed mouth. He fell off his elbow and lay on his back. Blood now drained down his throat. He gurgled. He coughed twice, geysering blood. Then he didn't cough anymore. No strength to blink–he died with his eyes open.

Myrna stepped around the body and went searching for a person of authority to report an attempted robbery.

Downstairs, Morgan finished writing to Lucas. She'd not heard the two pops one floor above. If she had, they failed to register as gun shots. She settled back in the swivel chair, away from the desk, and dropped her hands to her lap. Too late to post the letter today. He'd get the letter in a week or two. Lucas hadn't replied to the Christmas letter she sent three weeks ago. *Wish he would write more often*, she thought. It's all right, I guess, she told herself. Wouldn't want a mama's boy, but I would like to know he's safe wherever he is, whatever he's doing.

Morgan relished the time off for Christmas. She just didn't expect the idle hours would bring on depressing bouts of reflection. The months since she sold the mine in Bickford to Hearst, had flown by. The move to San Francisco, meeting George, and her work with him, (she was part owner of the mines) and Neville, all kept her too busy to think about much else. Now Morgan had time to ponder–where was she going with her life?

She would never marry Stryker. That man would never marry anybody. God, Morgan thought, she couldn't imagine living with him. What kind of woman could? Eventually, he'd be killed, anyway. Then she'd be no better off than she is now, a widow. And George, even if he weren't married, he's old. He doesn't have many years left in him. Both could die tomorrow.

Then what?

She had enough money to live on. The sale of the ranch and mine to Hearst took care of that. Money wasn't an issue. She also didn't know the $100,000 Hearst paid Stryker for collecting on a poker bet–*The San Francisco Examiner*–is in the bank, with her named as beneficiary upon Stryker's death.

Morgan rose from her chair and went to the kitchen cabinet. She withdrew her favorite wine and poured a glass. She didn't go back to the desk. Instead, she went over to a stuffed, comfortable chair, the only one in the apartment, and sat. She sipped from the glass. It was a good wine.

The fact that George would die soon was certain. You could see it in him. The man had lived a hard life, working years in the mines. Phoebe, his wife, it seemed in name only, seldom spent time with him. *Whose choice was that*? Regardless, he lived alone most of his life. Maybe that's why he likes Morgan's company. She liked the old man too. Actually, George was her kind of man, self-made. Younger? Yes, she might have married him, if he'd been single. But his life and hers were set.

Stryker was a different matter. A stronger feeling–was it only desire? No, but neither of them used the word *love* and they most likely never would. *What the hell is that, anyway? Is there something else, something just as strong, or even more so?* Her husband, did she love him? Passion was low, but the marriage was solid. *He was a good man. Can you love a man only for his virtue? Was that love?* With Stryker, passion goes through the roof. His energy, his power, yes, his power overwhelmed her. She's never felt such excitement. Is that love? Can a woman have what she had with Preston, her husband, and now have with Stryker in one man? No. It's like holding a rope around a pole. You pull one end, and what you gain must be given up at the other end. So, it's impossible to have both. *I wouldn't want both anyway.*

Suddenly, she stiffened. *What will Stryker do when Hearst dies?* His life was torn apart when his wife died and then murdering the man most responsible for her death. His work for Hearst gave him some stability. Between the missions, he spends time in Pescadero. Maybe he needs to. The violence, the killing, the living on edge–it all has to be offset with something. Pescadero must do that for him. But Stryker couldn't live in Pescadero all the time. *So, what will the man do?*

That line of thinking required another taste of wine. Morgan took a sip and paused, holding the glass in front of her. Studying it, she allowed herself a few thoughts about wine. Yes, the grapes were good. Certainly, she enjoyed each sip. Sometimes she'd swirl it between teeth and gums, or let it linger on her tongue before swallowing, savoring the taste of it. Eventually though, she'd consume it, take all the wine in the glass–she only allowed herself one glass at a sitting. Then it would be finished. But . . . she would enjoy the wine now. Maybe she'd have another wine in the future, perhaps on another day. Maybe, maybe not, but she'd make that decision in the future.

Morgan got up from the stuffed chair and set the half-empty glass on the table. *I need to put names on the packages while I still remember who I bought them for.* She hadn't bought one for Stryker. *You don't buy gifts for him.* She smiled. *I have something else in mind for that bastard.*

CHAPTER NINE

It started snowing again in Johnsville. Flakes fell gently, as if the weatherman wanted a perfect Christmas Eve. Not a threatening storm, the heavens sprinkled just enough snow to add to the holiday mood. Shadows grew longer, fainter, as gray clouds crept into the sky. Still, snowfall remained light even after the sun hid behind the clouds.

Stryker and Tooonug crossed Main Street and headed for the Johnsville Hotel to find Nicolas. Stryker failed to say where or why they were snowshoeing to the hotel. If Tooonug had any curiosity, he kept it to himself. The webbed shoes worked all right if a man didn't try to rush it. The townsfolk, some walking, but most of them gliding on longboards, allowed a wide berth for the newcomers, especially Stryker. Inside the houses, lanterns came to life, casting yellow glows in the windows, and outside, as the temperature dropped, scarves were wrapped a little tighter.

Nicolas sat at the letter desk. The dark mahogany desk was used by guests to write and post mail. Pouring over a list of names on parched paper, he didn't see Stryker and Tooonug enter.

"Let's talk," Stryker said, as he approached Nicolas.

"Ah, Stryker, I didn't notice you came in. Have you found out anything?" Nicolas folded the paper and laid it aside.

"Looks like older juveniles formed a cult."

"Why? Why do you think that?" Nicolas seemed surprised. He twisted hairs on his beard with thumb and forefinger.

"Events, I want to know about 'em," Stryker said.

"Events." Nicolas cupped his chin in the hand. "Well, there's usually a Christmas Pageant on Christmas Eve. That'd be tonight. Sometimes a few groups wonder about singing songs, Christmas carols. And of course, friends gather at each other's homes for partying, can go late. Why, what's going on?"

"Your gifts thing, when?"

"Later, after midnight, after houses go dark. I ride the sleigh and just leave packages on the porches."

"Tell me about tomorrow." Stryker eyed the eight young people in the lobby, wondering if any looked suspicious. The guests, males mostly, probably came into town for the races. They gathered in groups of three or more and talked among themselves. They seemed all right.

"Well, the races don't start until around noon. The snow's better earlier, but a lot of the fellows and women too, I guess, aren't too steady in the legs at that time," Nicolas chuckled. "And after the races, they kinda pick up where they left off the night before. It's Christmas, no working the mines, so everybody has a good time."

"Take someone with you tonight," Stryker warned.

"You worried something might happen?" Surprise burst on Sanford's face.

"I'll go with him," Venard said. He'd only heard the last part of Stryker's words. "Talkin' about leaving gifts for the kids, right?"

Stryker and Nicolas spun to see Luscious and Venard's approach. Stryker chided himself for not seeing them come in.

"Yes, yes, it is. But it's . . ." Nicolas protested.

"No. A gun hand, not a preacher," Stryker growled.

"We'll be fine. They wouldn't harm the man who brings gifts for children," said Venard.

"Listen to him!" Luscious cried out. "They killed two girls! Cut off men's heads! The preacher and a deacon, for God's sake!" She cried, then caught her breath. "Why is this town not doing something about it? Jesus Christ, are you all crazy?" She wailed.

"Oh, now, honey." Venard put an arm around her shoulder.

Luscious swept off Venard's arm. "Don't honey me! Want your God-damned head on a fence post?" Fire flashed from the baby blues. "Damn you, Venard!" She was plenty mad.

"I'm doing it," Venard declared.

"What'cha you doin' tonight, Stryker?" Asked Nicolas.

"Be around." Stryker said. He turned to Tooonug. "Stay with Nicolas." Stryker walked out of the hotel.

Luscious watched him go. She cooled a little. Tooonug helped. "We'll stay close to you too, Nicolas."

Stryker carried the snowshoes instead of strapping them on and headed to the school. Either he was getting used to walking on the slick street or he was unconsciously taking shorter steps, but regardless, his footing improved. He made it to the schoolhouse without slipping. Downstairs, where the classes took place, he saw nothing but empty desks and Dag's bunk. He heard movement overhead and took the stairs to the second floor. There he saw Gertrude re-making his bunk.

"Putting on clean sheets." Gertrude passed her hand on the top cover, pressing out the wrinkles.

Stryker waited for her to finish with the bed. The damn woman was one hard-looking bitch. "How long you know Bandy?"

She seemed surprised at the question. "We've been married a year, little longer, I reckon."

"Before that."

"Nothing, he got drunk one night, and we got married." Gertrude grabbed a mop that had been leaning against the wall. "Why you wanna know?"

"He a religious man?"

"Good gracious, no. Justice of the Peace did it. Why you asking that?"

"The killings, what's he saying 'bout them?" Stryker asked questions now. He needed answers in a hurry.

"He ain't said much. He–why you askin' these questions?" She let go of the mop and jabbed a forefinger at Stryker. The handle hit the floor with a crack.

"Figure he knows more than he lets on."

"Maybe I do too," Gertrude said. Her face remained stern, no hint of what that meant. She put her hands on her hips. "Yeah, mister, maybe I do."

"Tell me."

"Need to do a little checkin' first, then I'll tell ya." She bent and picked up the mop. "I'll come by after the pageant. You be here."

"You and Mandy live close by." Stryker said.

"On Arastra Street, two room house 'round the corner." Gertrude wagged her head to the right. "I live there anyway. Close to the school here. Mort stays at the jail most nights."

The grimness never faded, and Stryker got nothing from how she talked. He had to settle for what she said. Push her, he thought, and the strong will-woman might turn against him. He'd already decided to see Mandy again. It would not be a friendly visit. He'd wait and see what Gertrude came up with before he beat the shit out of Mandy.

Stryker weighed her reaction to what the woman might do and then posed the same line of discussion he'd had with Mandy. "People seem damn mirthful with what's been happening. Girls not from here, but the preacher and the deacon were. Folks don't seem that riled up."

"Them two was not all that well liked, a little too sanctimonious, maybe. The preacher, he talked a lot of Godliness in the pulpit. Some said he liked children a little too much and stole from the offering plate. The Butcher man, Carl, don't know much 'bout his doin's, 'cept he used to beat his boy something awful. You could hear it sometimes."

"That boy, first one to go missing." Stryker said.

"What I heard." Gertrude tightened a little.

"Describe his looks." Stryker was close to the line.

"He's a good-looking boy, okay?" She bristled noticeably now, as if she had it in for handsome men, especially those who turned away from her. You could tell it was a real sore spot. She calmed down, probably realizing she gave away too much. "Blond hair–he's an Adonis." She hit Adonis hard. "Don't ask me no more. See you tonight." Gertrude carried the mop to a pail by the door. She lifted the bucket, took one last look at Stryker, and disappeared down the stairs.

Stryker figured she'd had enough. A face like hers, she must have been hammered hard growing up. People can be cruel all right. He waited until he heard the front door open and shut before he went downstairs. He'd seen a dinner place advertising good food on Main Street. They all advertise good food. *What place advertises bad food*, he thought.

The sign read "Aunt Sue's–Good Food." The restaurant was a single-story building recessed a few feet from Main Street and next to the Italian Hotel. Four sleighs with a horse in front of each waited by the stoop. He went inside. Not very big, all eight tables covered with checkered cloths were occupied. In the far corner, a table with four straight-back chairs sat Dag and the Dhals. Stryker turned to walk out when the Dane called out.

"Stryker!"

Every eye in the place looked at Dag, then at him. He hesitated.

"Come! Come sit here!" Dag stood, waved his arm, and yelled the invite.

Stryker's belly made the decision. His last meal was more than a day ago. He wasn't just hungry; he needed to eat. He made his way between the bulky coats and jackets on chair backs to Dag and the Dhals and pulled out a chair. He scooted it around to where his side was to the door. Dag sat in Stryker's preferred chair, back to the wall, facing the door. Luscious sat opposite Stryker, between Venard and Dag.

Stryker felt the tension. Thick; he couldn't cut it with the straight razor.

The cause of it took place before he walked in Aunt Sue's. Nothing really, just an inadvertent touch and a not so inadvertent, very slight, squeeze of the hand. Dag called the Dhals to his table when they entered. Luscious chose a chair closer to Dag, pretending not to see Venard pull out a chair for her opposite Dag. Venard noticed the lingering glances, the smiles given too freely; the conversation being dominated between Dag and Luscious. Those things could have been harmless, maybe. But what happened under the table was different.

Luscious' spoon fell off the table. Shoved to the edge by the waiter, it tottered there until a knee bumped a table leg and sent it to the floor. Both Dag and Luscious bent to retrieve it. Dag had meant to gently brush her hand aside. He would get it. But when he moved her hand with an open palm, Luscious mistook the gesture. She squeezed his hand. Dag, though surprised, squeezed back. Neither looked at the other, and Dag retrieved the spoon.

But the moment lasted a little too long and when they came upright, it was obvious to Venard something happened under the table. Faces that were a little too red, nervous eyes that refused to meet, and a sudden loss for words betrayed them.

Venard let it go.

The room was cozy and festive, decorated for Christmas with wreaths and ribbons. It buzzed with loud talk and plenty of laughter. Most of the occupants looked to be in their 20s, an equal number of men and women. Clearly Aunt Sue's was a popular meeting place and Stryker figured they'd taken seats at Dag's table which were coveted by the other females.

"The food, it is crazy Swiss-Italian. It is very good if you get the Swiss. The Italian is probably good too if you get the Italian. I got the Swiss, which is also good." Dag smiled big and talked with his mouth full. But his accent added to the festive atmosphere.

Venard and Luscious said little. They ate quietly.

When the waitress arrived, Stryker ordered a plate of Polenta and Braised Beef. He wanted a beer but got coffee instead.

Dag continued talking of home in Denmark, and other topics of no interest to them, except perhaps to Luscious.

Dag drank from a big stein of beer. He noticed Stryker eying it and said, "If you race with a clear head, you go too slow. Besides, it provides ballast." He grinned big again. Then he erased it, leaned closer, and lowered his voice. "How are you doing with the killings?"

The Dhals leaned in to hear too.

"You've been here a while," Stryker said to Dag. "What've you heard?" Stryker was in no mood for small talk.

"Not much. They ignore. It is a festive time. I do not think the two dead men were much liked, and no one knows the two dead girls." Dag gulped the last of the beer and waved the empty glass for more. He lowered it to the table and shifted forward again. "I did hear of parties out of town. Young people, some go and come back. That's all I know."

By the time Stryker walked out of Aunt Sue's, night had fallen on Johnsville. He stood on the stoop, looked over the sleighs, and watched people flowing past him, many riding on the long snowshoes. Families, couples, a few singles, young and old, they all were going to the church pageant due to start in thirty-five minutes. He considered joining them, but he spied Nicolas and Tooonug passing through lantern light up the street. Tooonug carried his snowshoes and two Winchesters. When they got to him, Tooonug handed one of the guns to Stryker. Stryker took it as if he'd asked Tooonug to bring it. Tooonug gave it to him as if he had.

The Dhals came rushing out Aunt Sue's, Venard holding his wife's elbow. "We should've been there by now," Venard said, as the two of them hurried past the three men.

Stryker said nothing as they fell in with the mob headed to the house of worship on Church Street. Stryker and Tooonug carried their snowshoes and carbines. Hardly anyone paid attention to the armed white man and an Indian. Men commonly wore guns around town, a few even wore them to church, but when they did, it was accepted, although they sometimes got a few looks. Stryker and Tooonug were with Sanford Nicolas, the lieutenant governor after all. Almost everyone in Johnsville knew him. Nicolas was a good man.

They stacked their snowshoes with the long boards against the base of a side wall outside the church. It wouldn't be hard to find which ones were theirs. They were the only stubby, webbed ones. Stryker would have preferred the long boards, but he knew he couldn't master those quickly enough.

They entered the church.

Inside, people strutted down the center aisle outfitted in their finest, with colorful hats, shawls and long dresses on the women, and men in their best Sunday suits as they packed in the pews. Everyone came gussied up for the festive occasion. A couple of regulars made much of Nicolas's being there and insisted he sit on the front pew with them. He did. Stryker and Tooonug stood along the back wall.

Saint John's Methodist Church held over a hundred and seventy people if you put chairs in back and along the sides. The pulpit rested on the left of a three-foot stage. The elevated platform ran from side to side with enough room on each end for a short set of steps. A green curtain behind the pulpit stretched across the entire width of the stage. Flickering wall lanterns casting dancing illuminations on white-washed walls shined dimly on opened hymn books. Lanterns on four spoked wheels overhead provided additional light. Garland with red bows hung on each end of the pews. You could hear heavy pieces of the set being moved into place on the stage, and every so often someone would bump the curtain. Muted conversations droned in the congregation, interrupted by occasional, controlled laughter. People continued to file in as ushers searched for room in the pews.

The play, a re-enactment of the Nativity, was described in programs handed out at the door. Actor's names and ages were listed inside the single fold paper. All the actors had yet to reach the age of fifteen, and some were as young as five. The children took their acting parts seriously, and parents and close relatives scrunched tightly together in the front rows to see the young thespians. Friends, distant relatives, and those who just came to see a Christmas play sat in the middle rows. Older teenagers and stragglers took up the back pews. Some, like Stryker and Tooonug, stood against the back wall.

The Paiute was enthralled, attentive, and he craned his neck to see the stage. "White man do sacred dance?"

"No dance." Stryker scanned the crowd. No Chinese, even though Asians made up half the town. There were two wood-burning stoves for heat, but body heat from the crowd also kept it comfortable. Lots of gray and white heads in the pews, grandparents probably come to fulfill obligations.

"What they do?"

Stryker overheard people talking about the play, *The Birth of Jesus*, as they entered the church. "Son of God's birth."

"Sun God . . . birth." Tooonug nodded his head as if he understood.

"Watch the door." Stryker pointed the barrel of the .44-40 at the door. Two older boys on chairs lined up behind the last pew heard him and twisted around to watch the door too.

It wasn't Broadway, but it was big for Plumas County.

Finally, fifteen minutes past the announced start time, the new Methodist Reverend of Johnsville came out from behind the end curtain and stepped to the pulpit. The crowd hushed, except for a few females who hadn't seen Venard. Those women continued yakking until they suddenly realized they were the only ones still talking and everyone could hear them.

"My name is Venard Dhal, your new minister, and I am so happy to be here tonight!" He shouted with a wide grin. "And I'd like to introduce my wife, Lucinda, who's here too!" He pointed to her in the second row. "Stand up, honey."

Luscious stood, faced the crowd, and did a little dip. She smiled big too.

Men offered amens with broad welcoming grins. Women's grins, not so much. They offered frowns instead.

Undeterred, Venard went on. "I can tell by the excitement in here, you want the play to begin! So, let's get started!" Venard disappeared behind the curtain. A few moments later it began opening from the center.

The performance started with several shepherds in the fields watching over white cardboard sheep. They carried wooden canes and wore brown ragged clothes. An angel wearing a white robe with wings appeared and the men (boys) were so afraid. "Be not afraid," the angel said. "For unto you is born in the City of David, a Savior. He is Christ the Lord." Parents whispered names, pointed, and waved. The youthful actors waved back. Boy and girl shepherds who'd cowered on their knees, rose, and walked off the stage.

Next, the Three Wiseman appeared, young Kings of around twelve years' old, wearing crowns and long purple robes. They bore gifts, boxes labeled "Gold," "Frankincense," and "Myrrh" written in big letters on the sides. They stopped and chatted amongst themselves and one pointed to a star in the sky, which was actually a paper star hanging at the far end of the stage. Parents whispered names, pointed, and waved. The youthful actors waved back. The curtain closed.

Probably not over five minutes passed before the scream. It came from outside the church. It was more anguish than fright, and it came from a female. Stryker almost didn't hear it; conversations in the pews had grown loud. But Tooonug stood closest to the door, and he'd heard it too.

"I go see," Tooonug said. He spun with the Winchester gripped chest high and in three light, quick steps; he was out the back door.

Stryker edged closer to the door and remained inside. She cried out again, and he heard the wail more clearly. He tried to see through the door and into the night. But he couldn't see anything except the snow-covered ground in the dark night.

Her scream turned to sobbing. "Why would anyone do this?"

Then four shots rang out, first one, then two more within seconds of each other. The fourth shot came thirty seconds later, sounding distinctly singular.

Talk stopped. The gunfire quelled it. A woman in the second to the last pew silently mouthed a question to the man beside her, "What was that?"

Tempted though he was, Stryker remained by the door. He chambered a shell in the Winchester. People swiveled around, anxiously looking rearward. Four men, Sheriff Bandy and three others, miners probably–they looked like miners–got to their feet, converged in the center aisle and headed for the rear door. The four men wore side arms but hadn't drawn them. As they got to the door, Tooonug bounded up the steps.

"What happened out there?" The Sheriff asked, above church level.

Tooonug pushed his way between the men to Stryker.

Bandy and two of the miners hung back to hear what Tooonug had to say while the fourth stepped cautiously through the door.

"Kill donkey and sheep." Tooonug ran a forefinger across his throat. "They lay on snow, feet still move. Two boy and girl say they there to bring in church. One boy tell me shoot donkey and sheep, so I do. We see two men on snowshoe down street. They much hurry. I shoot. Hit one. He still live. They gone now."

Stryker started to say something, but just then Venard appeared from behind the curtain.

"Folks, there's been a slight disturbance outside. Nothing to worry about. We'll continue tonight's performance in a brief moment." He swept open the curtain and disappeared behind it.

"C'mon," Bandy said, leading the others outside.

"Stay here," Stryker told Tooonug, and he slipped to the other side of the door. Tooonug edged closer to the door, opposite from Stryker. They waited. Tooonug stood there, his face implacable as always, eyes staring black and cold. Stryker studied him, wondering if he was born that way. *Probably, and Gertrude too. I need to see that woman.* Several minutes passed and nothing more happened until Bandy came back.

The Sheriff glanced at Stryker and nodded. When Bandy spoke, he did it loud enough for many to hear. "We searched around the building and didn't see nothing. I left three men out there to keep an eye on things." He also left out the dead animals. "Let's get on with the play!" he shouted.

The Sheriff stayed in back by the door, next to Stryker. The woman who'd sat next to Bandy scooted into the empty space. She wasn't Mrs. Bandy; in fact, Stryker hadn't seen Gertrude in the church.

The curtain opened. Joseph and Mary who was with child walked across the stage. They stopped at a wooden wall with a door. The word "INN" was written above the door.

"Be back later," Stryker said.

Tooonug said nothing. He knew. He was to stay there and stand guard.

Bandy's eyes questioned Stryker's leaving. Stryker looked at him but didn't say anything, and Bandy let it go. When Stryker passed him, he returned his attention to the stage.

Stryker strapped on the snowshoes outside. He wouldn't be able to see tracks well at night and figured whoever killed the animals had left town, anyway. He wasn't searching for tracks, snowshoe tracks were all over the place. He was looking for blood, and if found, how much.

"Where's he goin'?" Bandy groused to Tooonug.

"He go out," Tooonug said. He stood with the Winchester in the crook of his arm, looking like one of those wooden Indians in front of a store.

Bandy shrugged his shoulders and watched the play.

Stryker found blood. At least it appeared to be blood. About two hundred paces from the Nativity scene at the corner of Arastra and Pine Streets, he saw dark blotches in the packed snow. Must have been using light from the nearby window to strap on his shoes, Stryker figured, and that's when Tooonug shot him. When he leaped or fell out of the light, Tooonug must have held fire. There wasn't much blood, but Stryker couldn't tell for sure once he stepped away from the window.

He gave up on the blood and retraced his steps to Church Street. He snowshoed past St. John's Church and cut over to School Street. Taking off the snowshoes, he stored them by the door. Downstairs was dark and appeared empty, hard for Stryker to know for sure. He called out Gertrude's name just loud enough to be heard if she were in the classroom. No answer. Upstairs turned out to be dark as well, but when he called out her name, he got a reply.

"Over here, Stryker."

She sat on his bed. "I've been waiting for you."

He couldn't see her clearly, even after he followed her voice to the bunk. He towered over the outlined shape seated on the bunk. "The gang, I want 'em."

"I have a favor." Her voice quivered.

Stryker thought about using force on her, but he held off–for now, anyway.

"This is a small town," she began slowly. She paused, and when Stryker said nothing, went on. She adjusted herself on the bed. "People talk." Gertrude cleared her throat. "You want information." She spoke firmly now, gathering resolve. "I want what only a man can give." She rushed it out, but her voice still cracked.

"Gertrude, you're . . ."

"Married? That's an excuse." She grew stronger, bolder. "But if I were . . . beautiful?"

Stryker had to admit he was stunned. He also had to admit she was right.

"Mortimer married me when he was too drunk to know what he was doing. He passed out that night before anything happened. I heard talk later he'd lost a poker bet."

Stryker let her talk.

"All these years, even my own husband . . ." She fought hard against the quiver in her voice. "You're new in town. You won't stay." She paused again. "You don't have to kiss me or hold me. I'll sit on you."

The information on the cult gang wasn't the only reason the mean son-of-a-bitch said, "All right."

"I'll move so you can lie down. Would you mind not wearing anything?" She said, as if it were a trivial matter. The bed springs creaked when she rose to her feet.

Stryker took her place on the bed and began struggling with a boot. Gertrude stood by the window. She waited until she could tell he was undressing to begin her own. He could barely see the outline of the woman, but he heard buttons as she popped them open and the rustle of her dress as it fell to the floor. Maybe it was the faintness of light, but her silhouette made her look smaller. He finally worked off the first boot and dropped it on the floor. He tussled with the second as he watched what he could see of her. For reasons he didn't try to understand, the outline of her splayed elbows as she undid the bodice caused a twinge in his groin. He dropped the second boot and took off his socks. She was naked. He couldn't see it, but he knew. She was waiting.

Stryker rose to his feet and flung off his coat. The shirt, Levi trousers, and long johns came off quickly. He was running behind.

When Gertrude heard the bed creak again, she came over. He lay on his back, giving room for her to sit if she wanted. She did.

Although he couldn't make out her features, but the image of her face, a face even a mother couldn't love, the harshness, the ugly grimness, burned in his mind. He couldn't help it. The woman had Tooonug's mug pasted on her. He readied himself for the rough caress of a drill sergeant. It was a tough fight to keep the sergeant out of his bed. That's how Stryker felt about Gertrude. She reminded him of a man, and he hated it, hated her for it.

But when Gertrude touched him, the sergeant disappeared. Her hands were tantalizingly light and delicate. Soft and gentle. She used her fingertips not to stimulate, but to explore. Gertrude had never known what a man would be like. Stryker was already semi-hard, and as she timidly caressed a penis for the first time, discovering, fondling, measuring, he grew rigid quickly. He sensed the awkwardness and the trembling of her hand–sometimes hands–sent electrifying sensations down his lower spine. She started light stroking up and down with one hand, again not for him, but for her. The woman was learning fast.

"Damn woman, it's getting hard to hold back!" Pre-seminal fluid leaked out, and she slickened his shaft with it. Stryker lifted a hand to stop her. He couldn't hold back much longer. But she stopped in time. The urgency eased. *Where's her other hand? What's it doing?*

Gertrude got up on her knees beside him and lifted a leg across his stomach. She placed her hands on his chest, not a lot of pressure, only enough for balance as she positioned herself over him. She eased down. Stryker felt the lips of her vagina, soft and wet, gently pushing on him. The angle wasn't quite right, and Gertrude pulled back a hand to help. But before the hand got there, he slipped in–deep.

"Oh!" She lifted off quickly. "Sorry." She tried again. He went in easily; rather, she took him in easily.

He remembered his first time. The crusty old sergeant told him he shouldn't die a virgin. At fourteen, he was the youngest member on the Parrott Rifle. Prostitutes from Sharpsburg slipped through the Rebel lines to trade their wares. Boys from the South had little money. Northerners had heavier pockets. Sarge gave the hooker a dollar. Rite of passage for Stryker, business for her, and it took all of five minutes. The sergeant died in an Antietam cornfield next morning. Stryker figured he wasn't a virgin, though.

Gertrude eased lower, careful and slow. She took a full breath, held it, and pushed down. No big deal, actually. He went through all right, couldn't even tell if she bled, although she was really wet. She released the breath. Still resting her palms on his chest, Gertrude started a rise and fall motion, being tentative, exercising caution. She never sped up, kept the same rhythm and speed. After a few trips, she began hesitating at the bottom, holding it, absorbing the fullness.

Hers was getting close now. The telling signs were there, urgency, strokes more demanding, signs . . . at least it seemed that way from what he'd learned from a few—okay, plenty of other women—and he wondered how she'd take it. Shaking, her entire body started shaking, that's how. She dug fingers in his chest and fell forward, spearing his chest muscles with damn sharp elbows. Stabbing pain in the pectorals kept his ardor in check. *Shit woman!* He gripped Gertrude's upper arms and pushed, lifted those bony weapons off his chest. She didn't make a sound. The whole time, Gertrude never made a sound. Embarrassed, he guessed. *You gotta let go, woman. Too bad.*

"Do it again," Stryker said, ordered. He pulled her close, crushing her breasts against his chest. That kept her clitoris rubbing on him. He urged, continuing by pushing and pulling on her arms. She went along with it and had another.

"That's enough," Gertrude said. Stryker released her arms. She reached for a towel she'd placed on the bed, waiting for his arrival. Using it, she cleaned him and then herself. She gathered her clothing without saying another word and moved away from the window to dress. Stryker reached for his own clothes.

As he pulled on his boots, Gertrude stayed in the dark where he couldn't see her.

"I heard the boys talk about a meeting at Fetzer's mine. It's an abandoned mine and shack roughly halfway to Mohawk. You'll have to climb up a steep hill left of the road. Half mile from it, I think. Fetzer claimed he found gold and tried to get money for it. He was a crook, and someone shot him. That's all I know." She rattled the words off fast and clipped as if they pained her. Maybe they did. Maybe something else did too. Maybe having to bribe a man to fuck her did.

Stryker left Gertrude standing in the dark. He should've held her, caressed her, said things you say during and afterwards, but he couldn't. *She would've shied away, thinking it was gratuitous*, he told himself. *Who knows? That asshole "Who" knows every God-damned thing.* Besides, he has other assholes to find and kill. He thumped his boots down the stairs as his goodbye.

CHAPTER TEN

In the church, Stryker tapped Tooonug on the shoulder and canted his head toward the door. Tooonug followed him out. "Grab your snowshoes." The two men snowshoed side by side to the stable. Tooonug didn't ask where after that. He would follow the mixed-breed, didn't matter where. No person was in the livery, Stryker figured they were probably watching the play. He lit a lantern and saddled the roan. Tooonug chose a bay mare. They strapped on snowshoes to both horses and led them out. Outside, Stryker and Tooonug tied snowshoes on each other's backs and they mounted up. The streets were empty as the two men rode out of Johnsville.

The snowing had stopped, the clouds having wandered off during the last hour. A full moon now shone brightly enough to grow shadows on the snow. Stryker glanced skyward. Weather can change quickly at higher altitudes. Even stars twinkled brighter tonight. After all, it was Christmas Eve.

They rode in silence. The horses' hooves made soft shushing sounds in four inches of fresh snow. They rode abreast for two miles before Stryker said, "If they're not all there, I want one alive to tell me where the others are."

"Keep two alive," Tooonug deadpanned.

"Look for tracks on the left, going up a hill." Stryker stifled his curiosity about Tooonug wanting a second man to talk.

Fifteen minutes later, Tooonug pointed left. Stryker had missed the signs. A broken pine branch lying on the ground was used to smooth out the parallel tracks, too smooth in fact. Even Tooonug might have missed the signs if the snowing hadn't let up. Natural curves and edges on the slope formed by the wind were also obliterated by the sweeping branch, and Tooonug's keen eye saw the unnatural shape, even in moonlight. If you looked farther up the hill, you could find where the tracks picked up again. The telling traces did not get missed by the skillful Paiute. Stryker did notice those who made the tracks traveled in single file.

They dismounted, put on show-shoes, and led the horses behind a clump of evergreens opposite the tracks. There they tied them.

"Bring rope," Stryker said. He pulled his own off the roan.

Both men carrying Winchesters at the ready started up the hill, following the tracks. It was quiet, and they stepped along carefully to avoid cracking ice or snapping a hidden branch. The snow would muffle the sound, but in the quietude of the forest even that would carry to a dog's or horse's ears, if one was by the cabin. But they couldn't quell their heavy breathing trudging up the hill. You could see the vapers in the moonlight.

Moving stealthily up the heavily wooded hill for close to ten minutes, Stryker and Tooonug crested a steep grade that leveled off to a small mesa of roughly a hundred yards or so before climbing again. They rested momentarily to catch their breaths. Then they saw the cabin. Not very big. It had two windows facing frontward and you could see lantern light inside. Smoke funneled up from a pudgy stone chimney. Stryker and Tooonug kneeled at the same time. No animals around, none could be seen anyway.

"Count the snowshoes," Stryker whispered.

Tooonug nodded.

Stryker rose to a crouch and moved forward cautiously. Tooonug followed. Fifty feet away Stryker could see two sets of snowshoes leaning on the wall next to the door. He held up two fingers to Tooonug behind him. Stryker crept on to the door. He turned to Tooonug, who crouched close behind him. "Don't shoot unless I do."

Stryker tried the lock, a wrought iron latch. He pressed down on the thumb latch. No click. He opened the door a hair's width. He nodded a go sign to Tooonug.

Stryker leaned back and shoved the door open with his boot. He fired a round into the cabin at the same time. He burst through the door as he jacked another round. "On the floor! Face down!"

Tooonug glided in behind, Winchester leveled.

It was a 20x20 one-room cabin with log cross beams supporting a V-shaped or gable roof. Six log columns, three on each side of the room, rose from the floor to every other beam. Bunk beds were laid out perpendicular to the side walls. A parsons table with straight-back chairs sat at the far end. A pot-bellied stove stood off center in the floor to allow the chimney pipe to extend to the roof, down and away from a center beam that ran front to back. The floor was bare except for a few mats on the floor. Lanterns hung on four of the columns.

Two scared-shitless boys threw hands in the air, a tall, lanky red-headed youth, struggling to grow facial hair and a shorter one sporting a black beard to match shoulder length head of hair. Shocked, they failed to comprehend what was happening.

Stryker stepped up to the taller lad and kneed him in the groin. The kid dropped to his knees. Stryker launched a boot in his ribs and the boy crashed on his side. He rolled onto his stomach. He was groaning pretty loud now.

The other boy, shorter, tougher looking, eased to the floor. Bare from the waist up–his shirt lay over a chair back–he had a bloody crease atop the fleshy edge of his right shoulder. He took his time stretching out on his stomach.

"What you gonna do with us?" The red head kid asked with the side of his face plastered to the floor. He sounded scared.

"Shut up, Jeremy." The other kid barked with his nose and forehead pressed against the rough boards.

"Wallace, I'm . . ."

"Shut up, I told ya!"

"Tie hands and arms behind. Leave enough rope to tie 'em standing to a pole." Stryker handed Tooonug the rope off his shoulder and backed up to the door. He took a quick look outside while keeping the carbine aimed at the two boys.

Tooonug worked fast. The Paiute knew how to use a rope. He threw loops around the boy's necks and tied their wrists high and tight on their backs, so that if they tried to lower their arms they choked. He then gripped the rope between the necks and wrists and pulled the tall boy to his feet.

"Aughhh! That hurts!" The kid sounded indignant . . . and he spoke with a raspy voice.

Tooonug dragged Jeremy to the nearest pole and tied him to it, looping one turn around his neck. He did the same with Wallace. Tooonug tied them facing each other.

Seeing no need for him to check on Tooonug's rope work, Stryker headed for the door. "Find out about the others while I look around."

Outside the cabin, Stryker could find no tracks except the ones made by the two inside. Two hundred yards higher up the hill he saw a black rectangular cavern in the moonlit snow. It looked like a cavity in the white hillside. He figured it to be the entrance of the abandoned mine. No light came from it and no tracks went to it. After a few more minutes of searching for more gang member clues, he turned back toward the cabin. That's when he heard what sounded like boots stomping on the floor.

He readied the Winchester and threw open the door. The stench overwhelmed him. He'd smelled it many times before—burning flesh. The first thing he checked rushing in was to make sure the boys were still bound to the columns. Tooonug, holding a hand shovel used to remove ashes from the stove, stood by Wallace partially blocking Stryker's view, but he saw the two boys remained secured as before. The Paiute glanced at Stryker, then returned to his task. Wallace's body sagged against the post, held there by the rope. His shirt had been torn in two and the sleeves were used to gag the boy's mouths.

Tooonug stepped aside and dug the shovel into the stove's red-hot embers. "He not talk." Tooonug pointed at Wallace, then at Jeremy. "He talk." Tooonug drew his knife.

Stryker saw why Wallace hadn't talked. He'd passed out. He'd either passed out . . . or died. His stomach was cut open above his belly button from side to side, the skin filleted out to form a pouch. The pouch was filled with hot embers. *Some marsupial.*

He'd brought Tooonug for the tracking. That was only the half of it. This was the other half. The savage knew how to punish, torture, and get information. It suddenly occurred to Stryker that Tooonug hadn't intended to waste time with Wallace. He used him. He tortured him for Jeremy's benefit. A staged play. That's why Wallace still had the gag in his mouth. He wasn't selected to talk. Jeremy was. Tooonug had performed the procedure as skillfully as a battlefield surgeon, detached and professional. Jeremy didn't applaud the play, his hands were tied.

Gotta hand it to Tooonug. Stryker cracked a crooked grin.

Tooonug approached Jeremy. The kid's eyes flashed wide with fright. He shook his head from side to side. He yelled something, but you couldn't understand him with the gag in his mouth. Tooonug took the knife, slipped it under the sleeve by Jeremy's cheek, and cut it loose.

"I'll talk! I'll talk! I'll tell . . .! Oh Jesus–Lord. What? What you want? Jeremy screamed. Then lower as he begged. "Please, please don't cut me. Please God." He cried.

Stryker moved next to Tooonug. The Paiute stepped back as if making a presentation–a whimpering, slobbering, quivering, mess. After what he just witnessed, he was now prepared to betray and crawl for his life.

"I want the rest. Tell me who, where, and what they're doing. The leader first–tell me now."

Jeremy, at age nineteen, had seen tough miners, tough loggers too, but none looked like these two. He saw no mercy, no sympathy, no feeling at all on their faces–cold, hard, death, not men–death. Jeremy now realized he would not live through the night. He wished they hadn't killed the preacher.

"Jack Butcher is the leader. He's called Mesiah. Two boys, Leaf and Dale. Three girls, Willow, Fawn, Dawn." Jeremy tried to sound factual.

"Where," Stryker growled.

"They went to Johnsville." Jeremy hesitated. He acted unsure. "They're gonna kill the new preacher."

"Tonight." Stryker said.

"Yes, I think so." Sounding more confident, Jeremy added. "Yes, tonight. You can leave me here tied up and come back if I ain't tellin' the truth."

Stryker switched the Winchester to his left hand and lowered it.

Jeremy exhaled a breath of relief.

Stryker closed in and pulled the sai. He brought it up by Jeremy's chest. The youth couldn't see it with his head roped upright. The center tine pricked the skin underneath the kid's chin.

"You're gonna cut me? I didn't lie!" Tears welled up again. "Please . . ."

Stryker bent at the knees and then powered upright with a violent thrust of the sai. The center tine drove up and through the base of Jeremy's tongue, and penetrated the frontal lobe. Jeremy's body convulsed violently two times. Then he died.

"Let's go, Tooonug."

Shit, Stryker figured, those boys killing the animals and returning to the cabin were probably meant to be a diversion. The two dead fools might not have known it, but they sure served their purpose. *Who's the fools?*

"Got to get back fast." Stryker broke into a run on the snowshoes. Tooonug loped easily behind.

CHAPTER ELEVEN

"You sure this is the right house?" Dale asked. He followed close behind Mesiah, assuming the role of second-in-command, and benefits the rank entitled. To Dale that meant the girl or girls Mesiah wasn't fucking at the time, he–Dale would get first dibs on who was left. It might even mean two of 'em. Leaf got sloppy thirds.

"Yes, dammit! Mesiah snapped. Now go knock on the door!" Mesiah, Leaf, and the girls stayed hidden around the corner as Dale crept to the front of the house and up the steps.

The Christmas play ended forty-five minutes earlier. At an hour prior to mid-night, Johnsville streets lay quiet, empty of its citizens. Those people still awake were either at home in bed, preparing for Christmas one way or another, or enjoying drinks somewhere indoors. Regardless, the streets were deserted.

"That must be Nicolas," Venard said, hearing the knock.

"I wish you wouldn't go." Luscious set up in bed to look at Venard.

He sat at the parsons writing desk in the upstairs bedroom. The prior preacher was a bachelor and would sometimes get up in the middle of the night to write his sermons. Venard left the desk upstairs.

He'd been working on next Sunday's sermon and hadn't gone to bed with Luscious. It would have been too hard to crawl out of the warm blankets with her in them. Besides, he already wore wool clothing and boots. His coat lay downstairs.

He set the pen aside and went to kiss her on the forehead. "I'll be back before you know it, darling."

"We've never been apart on Christmas Eve."

"Back soon." Venard turned and walked out of the room.

He heard more rapping on the door below, louder, sounding a bit angry. "I guess the lieutenant governor is getting impatient!" Venard yelled from the stairs. He bounded down the last three steps to the first floor. The stairs emptied to the hallway, a few steps from the front door. A double-wide doorway to the left led to a neatly furnished living room, four cushioned chairs, a coffee table, and two tables with lamps lit. No dining table. The former preacher took his meals in the kitchen. Venard went to the door and opened it. It wasn't Nicolas.

"Good evening, sir!" Dale shoved the door wider and barged in the house before Venard could protest or even return the greeting. Within a couple seconds, Mesiah, Leaf, and the three girls bolted up the front steps and poured in the room. Venard backed away.

"Who are you? What do you want?" Venard asked, keeping his voice low rather than yell out a warning to his wife.

"We're the welcoming party," Mesiah announced, stepping around Dale, his smile more malicious than friendly. "You're the new preacher, ain't ya?"

"Yes, I am." Venard retreated to the living room, away from the stairs.

The six youths followed him. Five encircled him, looking serious and threatening. Mesiah stood facing Venard outside the circle, still wearing a malevolent smile. He appeared amused.

Venard was unsure what to do. He figured they were for sure the cult killers. But were they just trying to scare him? No, he decided, they came to kill him just like they did the preacher and the deacon. He was trapped with no weapon. Even if he made it outside, he couldn't outrun them. Upstairs wasn't an option either. So he hoped. He waited for their next move. He didn't have to wait long.

Mesiah gave the sign, a simple nod. Knives were suddenly drawn and the five youths, boys and girls alike, attacked Venard like a pack of wild dogs.

They stabbed and slashed repeatedly, over and over again. No single wound was lethal, but the stabbing was relentless. He covered his head with his arms and bent forward for a desperate lunge out of the house. That simply exposed his back to even more vigorous assaults with the knives. The blades sank deeper.

Venard refused to yell, knowing what it would bring. Maybe they wouldn't look upstairs. His strength began to ebb, he stumbled. He fell to his knees, then on all fours. Willow leaped on his back, stabbing and slashing his neck. She was possessed. The stabbing, the blood, the killing, she'd become a crazed animal.

"Ride him, Willow!" Dale yelled. The rest stood back and watched Willow. They shouted encouragement and laughed.

Willow even kicked her heels in Venard's hips. Riding and stabbing, she yelled, "Yeee-haw!"

More laughter.

Venard finally collapsed on the floor.

"Hold his head up, somebody!" Willow waited until Dale and Leaf grabbed fistfuls of blond hair and pulled Venard's face off the floor. Then she began slicing his throat.

"Stop it!" Luscious screamed on the stairs. "You monsters! Oh, my God!"

"Whoa, baby," Mesiah exclaimed. "Look what we have here! Bring her to me."

"A gift for you, Mesiah." Willow pointed at Luscious with blood dripping from the knife.

Suddenly the room erupted in gunfire. A .44-40 bullet entered Willow's left eye. The large caliber bullet blasted a chunk of her brains out the back of her head.

Tooonug's round hit Mesiah in the shoulder. He spun halfway

round, yelped, and corkscrewed to the floor. Stryker and Tooonug rushed into the living room.

The remaining four dropped their knives. They backed away from Venard as if to show they had nothing to do with his killing. The bloody blades on the floor betrayed them.

"Venard!" Luscious clamored down the remaining steps and rushed to kneel by her dying husband. "Why?" She cried out. "Why?" She fell on his blood-soaked body and threw her arms around him.

Venard expelled one last frothy breath and went limp.

Luscious straightened, her face and nightgown soaked in blood. "Don't kill him." She pointed at Mesiah on the floor. "I want him." She sounded cold and menacing.

"Wait!" Dale screamed, flinging up his hands. We just came to scare him. Willow went crazy! She killed him!"

Stryker leveled the Winchester and fired. The bullet hit Dale in the chest. Stryker jacked another round and shot Leaf in the stomach. He gave the carbine to Tooonug.

Fawn and Dawn huddled together. "They made us come here! They made us do it!" Fawn wailed.

Stryker stepped over Willow's body to the girls.

"They kidnapped us," Dawn added, nodding her head in earnest. "Them boys did!" She pointed at Dale and Leaf on the floor. "They held us and . . ."

"They raped us!" Fawn screamed.

"And him, he's the leader." Dawn redirected her forefinger at Mesiah.

Mesiah lay on the floor groaning.

Stryker pulled the razor. He slashed both necks in a single rapid arc.

At first neither girl realized they'd been cut. The razor had flashed in a blur. But then a puzzled Dawn glanced at her friend and saw a red line begin to drape down her throat. "Fawn, you've been . . ." Dawn's warning ended in a gurgle.

Fawn turned and saw the look of terror on Dawn's face. She looked lower. Dawn had a red necklace. Horrified, Fawn tried to scream, but she inhaled blood, not air, and she gagged.

The girls staggered backward as they drowned in their own blood. Fawn fell to her knees and hung there, staring at the man who'd cut her throat. Dawn made it to a chair and sat.

Fawn settled back on her heels, taking short shallow breaths, and then she stopped. She tried to hold it–stop the bleeding, the drowning–delay her death. Then Fawn's brain shut down.

Dawn just sat, looking resolute. She coughed, spraying the folds of her dress. She coughed again, slumped from the chair, and died on the floor.

"What you want with him?" Stryker straddled Mesiah on the floor. He lifted the anointed one's chin and readied the razor.

"Please," Mesiah begged.

"Not that," Luscious said.

Stryker released his chin and stood up.

"Will you help me?" Luscious asked.

"Tooonug, help her. Tie him up with something first. Then do what she wants you to do."

The Paiute took belts from Dale and Leaf's bodies and bound Mesiah's wrists and elbows tightly behind his back. He wasn't gentle, and he ignored Mesiah's screams of pain.

Stryker walked out of the Parson's house and headed toward the Sheriff's office.

"Get your undertaker to the preacher's house," Stryker said to Mandy. The Sheriff first heard the pounding on the door in his sleep. It was like that inexplicable sound in a dream that won't stop. And then gradually you transition from the dream to consciousness and realize the sound is real. It was dark in the Sheriff's office and although Mandy heard the pounding on the door, it took him a while to figure out what it was. He remembered he should have armed himself about the same time he turned the doorknob.

"Shit, it's you." Mandy wiped his eyes with his sleeve. "What? Come in." Still struggling to organize his mind, he wasn't yet awake enough to be grouchy. He pulled out the chair behind his desk and sat. He fumbled for a match, almost knocked the lantern over trying to find it, and struck the match. The wick flickered to life. He placed his palms on the desk and leaned back. He acted as though his position behind the desk bolstered his authority. "What's happened?"

Stryker sat on the front corner of the desk. "The cult gang came in town last night, killed your new preacher."

Mandy suddenly straightened. "Dammit!" He yelled, slamming his fist on the desk. "How d'you know this?"

"Me and the Indian walked in on 'em at the parish."

"The wife?" Mandy asked, with a quick frown of concern.

"Not hurt."

"You said walked in on 'em."

Stryker nodded.

"Well, what d'you do?" Mandy fired the question quickly.

"Killed 'em."

"All of 'em? How many was there?"

"Eight. Killed five in the house–plus two more south of town."

"All kids?"

"Old enough to die young," Stryker growled.

"And one's still alive?"

"Wounded. Be dead soon." Stryker elected not to elaborate. Luscious needed to do what she needed to do. "Tooonug's with Luscious."

Stryker scooted off the desk and started for the door.

"Hey, wait a minute!" Mandy leaned forward to stand. But Stryker was gone before the Sheriff could extricate his butt from the chair. "Did you get their names?" He asked, the words trailing off to a whisper.

Outside the Sheriff's office, Luscious and Tooonug rode silently past Stryker on the same sleigh he and Tooonug had used. Mesiah sat securely tied to the rear seat. No acknowledgments were offered. Stryker stood and watched them ride out of town, going south. He briefly pondered where they were taking the youth. Wherever they were going, it would not end well for the anointed one. Tooonug's unique skills would be of immense help to Luscious.

Stryker continued down the street toward the school. *Never figured out the Sheriff's part in this*, he thought. Something was missing. Didn't matter now, though. The cult members were dead–except for Mesiah, and his death was certain–probably not as soon as the kid would like.

Job done.

Inside, Sheriff Mandy settled back in his chair. He sat there, staring out over his desk, staring at nothing really.

She'd been a saloon girl, a prostitute, pretty with red hair. He'd met Wanda in Jamison City. It was paid love. When she got pregnant . . . in the first place, he didn't know whose it was. She said the child was his. How the hell would she know? She followed him to Johnsville. But he refused to have anything to do with her. She went back to working and raised the boy on her on. As time went on and the boy grew, it became more evident the lad bore a strong resemblance to him, and Mandy learned his name. Still,, anyway he, respected man in the community, couldn't own up to a bastard son with a whore. That's the way it remained until a week ago. She came in his office and said the boy had disappeared. Been gone four days. Would he help find him?

He worried the boy had joined the cult, but he kept it to himself. Now, there was a chance he was one of the kids Stryker killed tonight. He secretly liked the lad, a hard-working youth, and he hoped Jeremy was all right.

Dag snored. The Dane had not stayed up drinking the night before the races. Stryker knew that because he heard Dag sawing logs in his bunk. Scant moonlight found its way inside the school, and Stryker ran his hand along the wall to find the stairs. Luscious and the Dane now? The edge in the woman's voice would seem to put that on hold. Maybe it would never happen. Grief crowds out other emotions. *Will that ugly woman be up there?* When he reached the top of the stairs, he saw from the window light the room was empty. He wouldn't have to decide, and he was bone tired, anyway. He barely got his boots off before reclining on the bunk and falling asleep.

Stryker woke, squinted at the window and saw gray dawn creeping in to start the new day. He remembered sitting on the bunk and laying back. Then he opened his eyes three hours later. There was nothing in between. He pulled on his boots.

The water that remained in the washbasin from the day before had a thin layer of ice on top. He broke it, splashed water on his face, and wet a forefinger to brush his teeth. After putting on his coat and grabbing the Winchester, he went downstairs. Dag sat on the bunk, applying dope on his boards. He looked up when Stryker stepped off the stairs to the floor.

"Morning, Stryker. Snow's wet today." There was no friendliness in the greeting. Dag had entered competition mode. He returned to the doping.

Stryker ignored Dag and crossed the floor. He opened the rear door leading to the outhouse and completed his morning duties.

Instead of re-entering the school, he hiked around front and gathered the snowshoes under his arm. He followed branches of packed snow trails along the streets to the Johnsville Hotel. It was time to leave Johnsville. Nicolas could ride with him, but he'd have to leave today.

Stryker found Nicolas sitting in a breakfast nook off the foyer. He was munching on a hefty chunk of pound cake while washing it down with a mug of coffee.

"Cult's dead. Time to go," Stryker said.

"Not going anywhere this morning. Next train out of Mohawk is three o'clock this afternoon." Nicolas placed the cake on his plate and cupped the mug in two hands. "It's Christmas, you know. I been up all night." He took a sip of coffee and then gulped it when he realized it wouldn't burn his lips. "After this, I'm getting some sleep." He returned the mug to the table and leaned over to shovel more pound cake in his mouth. He spit little pieces as he talked. "The races start at eleven. Watch them a bit, then go. 'Bout one o'clock'll get us to Mohawk in good time. You kill 'em?"

Shit. Stryker walked out of the hotel. He'd forgotten all about it being Christmas. Years ago, he'd celebrated the holiday with Leigh. Not since. Now breakfast was probably out of the question. Nothing would be open. Even leftover pound cake was most likely for hotel guests only. He didn't want it. He wouldn't take what wasn't his, anyway. *Shit.* He turned right outside and headed back to the school. The bunk offered much needed rest at least.

"Stryker!" Someone called his name a ways behind him down Main Street. Stryker looked around to see Sheriff Mandy hurriedly shuffling his way in the snow.

Mandy caught up to him, breathing hard. After huffing three more big ones he said, "That was one hell of a mess in the house." He paused for a comment from Stryker, which wasn't offered, then went on. "Them kids, they did all that stabbin' on the preacher?"

"Yes."

"Then, you shot three and the two girls . . . you cut their throats?" Without waiting for what he knew the answer to be, Mandy asked, why didn't you shoot them too?"

"They were last."

Mandy thought about that for a moment. "Them kids was from important families here."

"Show 'em Dhal's body."

"You seen my wife?" Mandy apparently figured he'd gotten all he could on the murders.

"Last night."

"She ain't brought my breakfast over to the office. Was coming to see where's my steak and eggs."

Talk of breakfast teased an empty stomach. "Any place open," Stryker said, asking, as usual, in a statement.

"Sammy's." Mandy hooked a thumb toward the south end of town over his shoulder." You gotta like chink food though."

With that, the two men parted in opposite directions.

Stryker figured noodles and stir-fry were better than nothing. He spied the china man's eatery about two hundred paces down the street on the right. *Fuck your wife every once in a while, Sheriff.*

He smelled it fifty feet from the door. His nose and stomach had a heated argument. He sided with the stomach and went inside. And there sat Dag. Four tables, three filled with Chinese eating noodles with chopsticks, and a table with one person alone, the Dane.

"Hey, Mister Stryker!" Dag waved him to the table.

Hunger prevailed. "Dag."

"Got to have energy for the races." Dag stuffed a forkful of drooping noodles peppered with bits of chicken, peas, and carrots into his mouth, stretching the limit of a hinged jaw. He chewed twice and swallowed half the squirmy load down his throat. "You order at the counter and bring to the table." Dag pushed the second half down his gullet as he loaded the fork again.

Even after watching Dag eat, Stryker was still famished. He gave the tiny Asian female at the counter his order by pointing at Dag's plate. No sense in taking a chance on what else might come from the kitchen.

"You catch the young killers?" Dag asked when Stryker returned with his plate.

"Yes."

"What's Johnsville going to do with them?"

"Bury 'em."

Dag set the fork aside, leaving his forearms resting on the table. "You catch all?"

"Figure eight was it."

"The minister's wife, she is . . .?"

"Gone, they killed her husband."

The races started on time. Stryker snowshoed to the mining mill at half past ten. Men with their long boards climbed in ore bucket ski lifts hanging from cables (Rumored to be the world's first ski lifts) and rode to the top of the hill. Several women, wearing dresses and carrying their boards, scrambled into the buckets as well. The hill was a steep slope of nearly eighteen-hundred vertical feet. The crowd by that time numbered in the hundreds, with the spectators lined up on both sides of the racecourse. Hardy individuals stretched the lines almost a third of the way up the hill. Several pockets of men gathered a short distance from the spectators, placing bets which ran into the hundreds of dollars. Today's purse for the overall winner stood at twelve hundred dollars.

Most of the hills around Johnsville were scalped, the trees cut to provide lumber for building the town and timber in the mine shafts. The racecourse was cleared of stumps and the steep slope lay as one long smooth white, rectangular blanket. On top, a banner stretched across the hill with "START" written on it, and at the bottom where most of the spectators clustered, another banner read "FINISH."

The sky was blue and the morning air crisp, a perfect day for snow-shoe racing.

"Most of 'em get drunk 'fore they get in the buckets," Nicolas said, coming up next to Stryker. He'd spotted the tall man among the crowd and made his way over to join him.

"They go that fast," Stryker mused.

"Close to a hundred miles an hour racing down that hill."

"Jennings is gonna take the Dane this year," Stryker overheard one of the men in front of him say to another.

"You got money on that?" His friend asked.

"No."

"Then shut up."

"Want to give it a try, mister?" A hefty male spectator behind Stryker and Nicolas, who'd overheard the conversation, asked.

"Too scary." Stryker spied hot cider being sold at a make-shift bar set up outdoors and wandered over to get in line.

"Big man's afraid," the man chortled to Nicolas.

Nicolas turned to him. "There's nothing on earth, heaven, or hell that man fears. You best move along."

"That right? Well . . ." He stopped in mid-sentence and got a good look at Stryker's face when the mixed-breed gazed his way.

Without another word, Hefty disappeared into the crowd.

The horn blew to start the first race. Racers at the starting line couldn't be seen from below. Stryker figured the hill leveled out on the crest. But a moment after the horn sounded, two racers appeared, sliding their long boards over the edge. Each man furiously pumped an eight-foot pole between his legs, pushing each thrust into the snow behind. The racer's fifteen-foot boards picked up pace quickly, and they stopped pumping the poles. They held the poles horizontally between their legs and bent at the waist to be aerodynamic. The long boards weren't made for turns. They were made to go fast, and they zipped side by side down the steep slope at ever-increasing speeds.

Stryker saw the man on the right pull slightly ahead. Then the other racer tried to push with his pole, lost his balance, and crashed. All you could see were arms, legs, and boards churning in a cloud of swirling snow. He came to rest and didn't move. The survivor crossed the finish line in triumph, greeted by a loud cheer. He slowed by dragging the rear end of the pole behind him, and as he did, it threw up a giant rooster tail of snow. The race lasted seventeen seconds.

Several men rushed up to the fallen racer, and Stryker wondered how many broken bones they'd find. To his surprise, the man was helped to his feet, shaken, but seemingly not seriously hurt. An even louder cheer erupted, and the loser hero waved to the crowd.

Stryker watched race after race. Mostly men, but a surprising number of women too. The winners climbed in the ore buckets for another race. Elimination races, and Stryker saw Dag win and climb in the buckets several times. The roar rising from the spectators grew louder with each race. With the alcohol consumed, the three makeshift bars had to restock twice.

×

Not every citizen in Johnsville attended the races that day. A small contingent of adults, parents and close relatives, gathered at the Johnsville morgue. Sheriff Mandy and the mortician stood in the room with them. The parents had come to identify bodies. As sheets were pulled off each of the deceased's faces, there was much wailing, shrieking, and cursing, yes cursing. Fathers and two of the mothers swore revenge on the man who'd killed their children.

The Sheriff waited a few minutes after the last child was uncovered and then he drew the sheets back over their faces. The weeping and yowling abetted somewhat, but the swearing continued.

"Come over here," Mandy ordered. He brought everyone to one last corpse. Had them gathered round as he uncovered Venard's entire body.

"This is what your babies did."

The multiple stab wounds had bled through the clothing. Venard remained alive during the initial attacks, and he bled profusely. His head lay at an odd angle though, nearly separated from the body, connected by the vertebrae and a single thread of ligament. The near capitation was what finished him off.

"Now shut up and go home."

The final race was announced. It would be between a nineteen-year-old miner named Karl Jennings or Jenner and Dag. Boisterous shouts of encouragement to Jennings roared up the hill. He may have even heard them. Those who had hung away from the ropes, talking with friends and neighbors, now crushed forward to see the race. Excitement electrified the air. There was lots of laughter and good-natured jostling as children squeezed between adults and kneeled by the ropes–everyone was having a good time.

Stryker, standing back and watching the spectacle, was struck by it all. He'd never seen anything like it. Strange behavior, he thought, the way they were acting. Throughout his life, hardship, tragedy, and death constituted his environs–certainly, nothing like this.

This Christmas Day, Stryker was witnessing for the first time people having fun. Having fun, he realized he'd never had fun. His life was antithetical to it. He'd never laughed and never experienced joy. He also realized he never would. His tree had grown crooked.

The horn sounded. Dag and Jenner crested the top of the hill.

Jenner pumped furiously as Dag executed long, smooth and powerful strokes with the pole. Down the hill they came, Dag now in a clean tuck and in the lead. Jenner, who'd stopped working the pole, started again. With each pole thrust his boards slipped side to side, not like Dag's which ran straight and true. Dag's lead was at least two board lengths over thirty feet.

But at the halfway mark, the lead was twenty feet. Then, with only two hundred feet left, Dag's lead shrank to ten feet.

Dag caught a glimpse of Jenner's boards edging up out of the corner of his eye. Dag started using the pole. For a while, neither man gained on the other.

The crowd of course was delirious.

But Jenner's youth prevailed. Even though his strokes were inefficient, and his boards advanced in jagged lines, he began to gain.

The racers crossed the finish line with the tip of Jenner's boards clearly in the lead by a half foot.

It took quite a while for the spectators to find their hats. Some got tossed as high as forty feet. And when a miner is festively shit-faced, a lot of hats look alike.

Dag, being a good sport, congratulated Jenner with a hearty handshake and hug. He held the boy's arm high in a victory salute, and hats were tossed again. The cheers for Dag were almost as loud as Jenner's. And although he had come in second, Dag won admiration and acceptance. He bought no drinks that day, but he got really drunk–shitfaced, in fact.

Younger kids jumped in the buckets and went up to ski down. Others got into a huge snowball fight. Men still hung around the snow bars and drank. Women gathered in clumps to talk. But spectators leaked off the hill.

"Okay, Stryker," Nicolas said to him. I suppose we'd better be getting down to Mohawk.

The mixed-breed took one last look at the hill. "Yeah, let's go."

They rode in a horse-drawn sleigh with the roan roped behind. Horses wore snowshoes. They'd gone four miles when Stryker noticed something up ahead and a few feet from the trail. It appeared to be the shape of a person sitting huddled in the snow. Stryker, who'd been the driver, brought the sleigh to a stop. He stepped out. Nicolas at first wondered why because Stryker had said nothing. Then he too saw the figure, but remained in the sleigh. Eschewing snowshoes, Stryker waded through thigh depth snow to who he now recognized as a woman. She wore no coat and sat motionless, wearing only a dress, the dress she'd worn the night before.

Stryker touched her face, a face covered with an icy veil that made her look peaceful, bridal, and even pretty. Gertrude was dead, her body frozen. Her head bowed, her arms folded, it seemed as if she had simply sat down and died.

"That a woman frozen dead sitting there in the snow?" Nicolas asked as Stryker climbed in the sleigh.

"Yes."

"Luscious?"

"No."

"We just gonna leave her there?"

"Yes."

Nicolas swung around to study the frozen figure as Stryker snapped the reins. "She must have gotten drunk and didn't know what she was doing out here. Stupid woman, she deserved to freeze to death."

"Shut up, Nicolas."

The two rode in silence the rest of the way to Mohawk. Even after boarding the Governor Stanford waiting for them, Nicolas chose not to ask his brooding companion any questions. Didn't matter, Stryker went to Johnsville and stopped the kidnappings and murders. He accomplished the mission like he usually did, killing everyone who got in the way and then letting God sort 'em out.

Stryker and Nicolas did sit next to one another in the coach. Nicolas read the *Examiner* making use of the remaining daylight, and Stryker watched the landscape float by out the window.

Eventually, the paper slipped lower to rest on Nicolas's round belly and he drifted off into a peaceful slumber, breathing regularly, snoring slightly. It had been a long night delivering the presents.

Stryker remained awake, staring out the window, even when it'd grown dark. The train engineer blasted the horn coming into Truckee, but Nicolas stayed asleep. He only shifted his rump on the seat. Stryker's brain reeled off several contemplations. Weighty thoughts wandered into his mind and lingered, some were analyzed, some simply observed. None gave him comfort.

Gertrude–what was she doing out there?

Luscious–he had no idea where she went with Tooonug and the wounded cult leader. She obviously didn't feel a need to see her husband's body again. Who would? Stryker never ran across Luscious again. *What'd she and Tooonug do with Mesiah?*

Two and a half years passed and three young boys were out on a long hike, exploring an old game trail. It led into a remote area that was a few miles west of the Mohawk to Johnsville trail. Heavy thickets of briar bushes made it almost inaccessible. The thorny bushes must have grown over the trail after its usage fell off. Curious and adventurous as teen boys often are, the three lads crawled under a hundred feet of prickly bushes and continued following the trail. It led them lower to a box canyon, guarded by large granite boulders. The now feint path wound its way between them to a spring surrounded by ponderosa pines. A beautiful, idyllic spot. They stopped to rest and munch on snacks before heading back, and one boy stepped behind a large boulder to relieve his bladder.

"Holy shit! Come look at this!"

The other two came running. "What?"

"Up there."

"Is that a man?"

"Yeah."

"What's he doing hanging on the tree"

"He ain't hanging."

"He fall from a cliff, get stuck up there?"

"No, ain't much left of him but look closer."

"My God."

"Yeah."

"He's been crucified!"

Good news in Truckee. The tracks were clear over the hill. The Governor Stanford pulled out of Truckee at 9:46 p.m. that evening. Stryker, next to the snoring Nicolas, and nothing to see but his own shadowy reflection in the window, tried to sleep. It seemed a lot less exciting covering the same rails, even after accounting for going in the opposite direction and moving slower uphill, when the rails were clear. The Stanford climbed steadily for three hours and rolled to a gentle stop at the Cardwell to take on fuel and water. The fireman came through the coach and asked if Nicolas and Stryker, the only passengers on the train, wanted to stretch their legs and get coffee. No food at this time of night, he said. Another hour and they rolled off the summit, heading west and downhill. Nicolas slept soundly and Stryker dosed fitfully until morning.

When they reached Auburn at 7:35 a.m., Nicolas sent the firemen to town for egg sandwiches while he and Stryker waited in the coach.

They made two more stops in Sacramento and San Jose, and rolled into the Ferry House station at 5:55 p.m. the day after Christmas reasonably rested and fed. Nicolas and Stryker took a horse-drawn cab instead of a cable car to the Palace Hotel.

Nicolas did most of the talking to Senator Hearst. Stryker had already informed Nicolas on the train that all the cult members were dead. Hearst glanced at Stryker when told about the killers with Stryker nodding in agreement. Hearst poured three glasses of good whiskey and raised his glass in a salute for a job well done.

"Sanford, I reckon you'll be spending the night and leavin' in the morning."

"Yes, and oh, before I go. Here is something for the lady I met here before we left." He held out a package to Hearst.

"Give that to Stryker," Hearst said. "He'll see her first. Stryker, your room's *424*, fourth floor. Deliver the package to *428*."

After taking time to bathe and shave in *424,* Stryker rapped three times on door *428.*

"Hello, Stryker." Morgan's smile was a combination of warmth and relief. "Come in."

Stryker handed the gift to her as he walked into the room.

"I didn't get you anything," Morgan said, closing the door.

"From Nicolas. Card there too." Stryker pointed to an envelope stuffed under the wrapping string.

"I'll open it later."

"No, open it." Stryker sat on the four-poster bed. Morgan had map rolls stacked on the only chair.

Morgan joined him, opened the envelope, and pulled out the card. "Hope you can find a good use for these. S. Nicolas," the card read. She unraveled the strings, tore open the brown paper, and opened the box. "It's a box of scarves, a half dozen, all different colors. Very thoughtful. Not sure where I'll use them though."

"Well...," Stryker said, lifting out one of the silk scarfs, and checking its length. He recalled an encounter with a woman named Layla in Ah Toy's House of Pleasure, located in Chinatown. Started out against his will, but . . .

He suggested a use. Morgan reluctantly agreed. Intelligent girls are more adventurous, often open to new things. *Morgan is extraordinarily intelligent.*

Ten minutes later Morgan lay naked and spread-eagled on the bed. Wrists and ankles bound to the posts with the silk. A pillow was placed under her hips, making a helpless presentation of her charms. A black scarf tied around her head covered her eyes. One scarf left. Stryker, being no dummy himself, used his imagination.

At first, he ran the scarf around her face and under her chin. Then he dragged the scarf around Morgan's bare shoulders and upper chest area, letting the tips float against the skin. He ran the ends around her breasts, occasionally leaning down and blowing, letting the silk tips flutter against the nipples, teasing them until they grew rigid. And he dragged the ends down her belly, blowing there too. Sometimes he pulled the scarf away completely, leaving the blindfolded Morgan guessing where he'd tease her next. The inside of her parted thighs also received attention, as well as where they joined farther up. There he allowed the tips to linger longer, and he moved his mouth close to blow on the ends of the scarf.

When he straightened to bring the scarf up to her face for another round, he noticed Morgan straining and pulling on the silk which bound her. She hadn't said a word. She didn't have to. Obviously, the scarfs were effective. He made another round. And when he came to where the thighs joined, he leaned down and flicked his tongue there several times. That elicited a guttural groan.

He lay next to Morgan and kissed her. She hungrily opened her mouth and kissed back. As they kissed, he brought his hand down between her legs. She was wet–damned wet. He moistened his fingers and gently caressed her clitoris. Bringing her along slowly, he let her have the first orgasm that way. He trusted the silk would hold.

Then he moved on top and entered her. With her pelvis tipped upward by the pillow, her clitoris didn't receive full contact, but that was okay. Morgan was satisfied for the time being, feeling him inside, moving in rhythmic strokes.

After a while, though, he pulled the pillow and re-positioned her hips. It didn't take long for her to have another orgasm. Then another a little later.

"Untie me," I want to hold you.

He did, and they continued until Stryker could hold back no more.

They rested for a short time, and it was well into the night when Stryker and Morgan admitted they'd had enough and fell asleep.

The next morning, Morgan lay with her head on Stryker's chest. "You going to Pescadero soon?"

"This morning."

"Okay."

Stryker left before breakfast. Morgan was a good woman, but for some reason he'd not felt totally right last night. It was as if he hadn't given his all to her. He should have held her longer, told her things. Spent more time with her. Maybe he'd visit San Francisco before long and make up for it. *Why not stay longer with her now?* But he didn't. He left the city.

Not until he was on the trail to Pescadero did he realize what was gnawing on him inside. It'd been lurking in the back of his mind, refusing to go away. Now, as he rode the roan, he knew.

It was that ugly woman sitting alone in the snow. Alone . . . wearing an icy veil of frozen tears.

ACKNOWLEDGMENTS

Thanks to a good friend, Stan Angle, who read all my books and gave me encouragement. RIP Stan

And special thanks to my long suffering editor who has to edit Stryker's mayhem--Stacey Smekofske

ABOUT WES RAND

Wes Rand was an Artillery Officer in the U.S. Army during the 1960's. He pays alimony. He doesn't like to golf but lives on a golf course. He has been bucked off a horse and two women.

He has a cabin in the mountains where he writes and hikes while his wife plays golf in Las Vegas. Wes enjoys living under the open skies in Nevada and Utah.

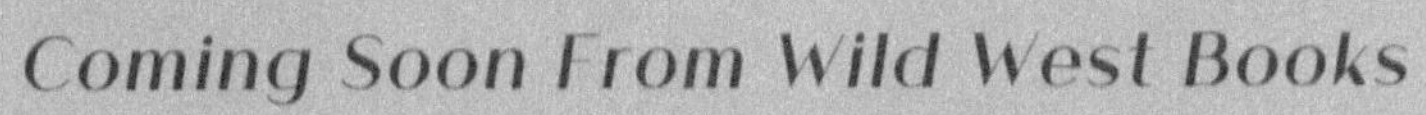

Coming Soon From Wild West Books

TROUBLE IN TAHOE

Book 6 in the Evil Stryker Series

LOOK FOR IT IN 2021.

www.ingramcontent.com/pod-product-compliance
Lightning Source LLC
Chambersburg PA
CBHW030746110726
47900CB00008B/2471